There's No Time!

THIS MAGAZINE IS FROM ANOTHER TIMELINE,
where John's life was affected by a drawing. Many similarities
exist. The drawing is the same. The effect was very different. This is
FRAGMENTA EIGHT.

EVEN AS THIS WORK INSTANTIATED IN OUR TIMELINE,
it, too, has changed. A magazine with a UPC code on the back cover?
Don't be fooled! Much of what you read here happened in both
timelines. Careful! If anyone asks what you are reading, tell them . . .

THIS IS ONLY AN AD!
It promises answers, like any other ad, but these are the REAL answers! DO
NOT let on that you have in your hands a document from another timeline!
The repercussions are simultaneously unknowable and likely terrible. Has
anyone ever come out any better for reading

SOMETHING THAT SHOULD NOT BE?

Be bold. Stay calm. Look natural. It's too late for you, but you can act. There is
knowledge to be had here. It may consume you, but them's the risks, cousin. You need
to decide what it all means. Don't assume we're here to help. It's all here, but where does
it go from there?

MARK THESE DATES NOW
SEPT. 15-16-17, 2000

for the Greatest Telekinesis Workshop Ever!

EARLY HANSELER
FOURTH ANNUAL HEALING CONCLAVE

*focusing on the BODY
in New, Fully Refurnished Location
Historic Maxwell Rouse Hotel
near the omphalos*

★TULSA, OKLAHOMA★

Featured speakers include esteemed psychic practitioners and diagnostic diviners. MEET AND HEAR THESE FEATURED HEADLINERS ...

Marla Hought, the bronchial telekinetic wild child loosening up pneumonia blockage with the power of her mind . . . **Figo Mastoric**, the cancer astrologer using the stars to predict the path of metastasis . . . **Siene Sarumoto**, author of *Hit Points Are Real* and a whole-body psychic healer of worldwide renown . . . **Edwald Hessergarten**, spirit consultant with history's greatest medical minds and the author of *Bleeding Isn't Always Bad For You* . . . **Sharina Piedpointe**, inventor of the Orgone Screwdriver and Tantric STD Healing Expert (Author of *Sex Those Scabs Away*) . . . **Garland Ferndale**, Canada's own psychic dermatologist . . . **Petra Shoskot**, the only living graduate of M.I.M.D., the Minsk Institute of Brain Action (*Minskiy Institut Mozga Deystviy*) . . . **Teskur Hamslop**, author of *The Mind-Thumb Connection* and *What Moves Around Inside You Can Learn*.

Every workshop will be a full house, so register early! The world telekinetic healing community will descend on Tulsa to share knowledge and learn what their colleagues have been up to since Charleston. It's never too early to register, so make your workshop reservations NOW! Many require special materials to be brought to the site, so don't be unprepared! Make your room reservations at the Historic Maxwell Rouse Hotel. Be sure to specify the one near the omphalos, so as not to get the one by the airport. Clip the coupon below and mail TODAY! There's so much to learn and share! Don't miss it!

you will not...

TIRE

you must not...

June 2000 | **Vol. 80 - No. 1** | **Issue 949**

ARTICLES AND STORIES

FEATURES

Editor In Chief.....**Ruth Corley Watt**   Circulation...........................(OPEN)
Guest Editor........**John Ira Thomas**   Adv. Prod. Mgr....................(OPEN)
Advertising Director............(OPEN)   Advertising Representatives:
Art Director.........................(OPEN)   New York City.....................(OPEN)
Designer.............................(OPEN)   Los Angeles........................(OPEN)

We do not accept responsibility for the return of unsolicited manuscripts, photographs, or artwork as it turns out there's a ton of all that lying around the *TIRE* office. If your story about your perfect enlightenment was so great, you should have made copies. Subscriptions no longer available, for reasons that will become obvious with the next issue.—JIT

Published just this one time by CANDLE LIGHT PRESS, 1470 Walker Way, Coralville, Iowa 52241. See page 130 for copyright information.

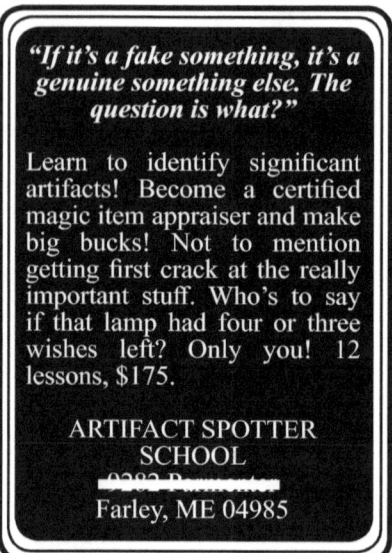
A Word to the Seeker

This issue of *TIRE* marks eighty years of publication. It was started by my grandfather, Carter Corley, as a trade journal for the tire business he loved. He worked hard at making it a beacon of excellence in the industry. *TIRE* was exceeded in circulation only by *THE JOURNAL OF RUBBER AND TREAD SCIENCE*, which often veered off into massive letter column battles and lacked much in editorial direction. *TIRE* was different. It was a sane voice in the wilderness.

When my grandfather passed away, my father, Arthur Peyton Corley, took a different view toward the empire his father had built. In a protracted legal battle with his father's estate, my father had attempted to dismantle and sell off what he called the "business part" of the business in an attempt to free himself of what he saw as material burdens. My father didn't see the tire business as an impediment, so much as something he didn't want to worry about. Carter Corley, seeing this urge building in his son from an early age, had crafted a Last Will and Testament with the intent of protecting the business part of the business from what he saw as wholesale destruction. He entered into this legal quagmire with his eyes wide open, despite the existence of two daughters eager to continue the business as originally conceived.

After three years of battles, my father got an allowance, and the only part of my grandfather's legacy that he could pry off of the estate: *TIRE*. As a part of his carefully-constructed last will and testament, Carter Corley left his only son Arthur a purely symbolic job with a modest budget. He was to become a Community Outreach Liaison. My father was supposed to hand checks to soup kitchens and smile for pictures in the Beacon Journal. The job was defined in the will with some care, but the divide in understanding between father and son had left an unexpected opening. My father had a different take on community outreach, and he came by it honestly, not as a calculated strategy. This was the only thing that all the strictures and codicils and probate hearings couldn't thwart—a true believer. Declaring the world to be one community seeking enlightenment together, my father made the case that he needed a way to speak to this world community as a single entity. *TIRE*, he argued, was that way. Without it, the job's requirements as set out in the will could not be fulfilled. The judge agreed with him. At the time, it was seen as an acceptable loss by my grandfather's lawyers. *TIRE* was all my father wanted, and both sides thought it had ended there.

The tiniest of legal victories resulted in unexpected consequences lasting twenty eight years. Carter Corley's carefully interwoven directives became a Chinese finger trap. Because of the careful wording of Carter Corley's will, the CEO of the entire business had to also be the editor in chief of *TIRE*, as well as head of all the other far-flung parts

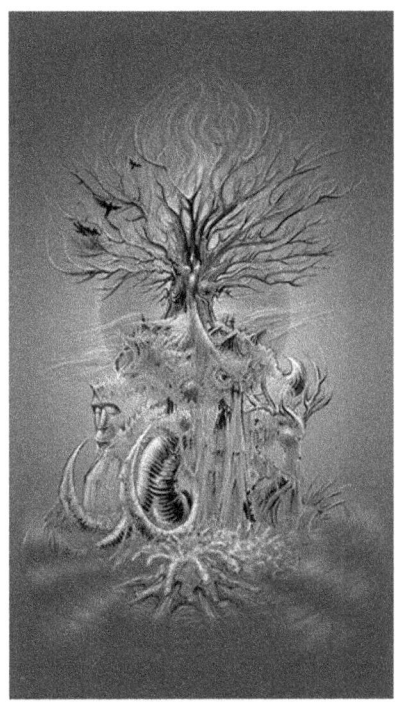

The Tree That Connects Us
LEARN ITS SECRETS!
Are you a root or a branch?
A berry or a leaf?
WHAT ARE YOU?

What is the connection between a handkerchief and the formation of stars?

Did you know that a hanky tied around a doorknob keeps spirits from passing into a room? Earthbound spirits can appear limitless in their access because of their intangibility. But they are earthbound in their thoughts. If they can pass through walls, why doesn't the Earth simply spin away from them while they shift through the void of space?

It's because they believe they walk the Earth as Men do!

The power of their belief moors them to the planet. Earthbound spirits, even when they appear to act in our interest, are ultimately unwelcome and must be exorcised. Where there may be one friendly ghost, there will soon be a poltergeist or worse. Despite what you see in movies or books, an earthbound spirit cannot ascend or descend if it avoids its opportunity to leave this plane of existence. Some manage to cheat another spirit at the moment of another body's death and take the journey set out for another, leaving that cheated spirit inside a dead body. This, of course, is how zombies are made. Other spirits will go so far as to arrange the death of a mortal to speed things along.

These malevolent intangible killers are all around us.

Have you ever cheated death for a moment and thought someone must be looking out for you? No-one is looking out for you. Just the opposite. You just avoided a malevolent spirit! What can be done? Locking earthbound spirits out of your home with hankies is a good start, but you have to go out sometime. Hematite pendants and exorcisms can work for days or months, but they are not permanent solutions!

Earthbound spirits must be disabused of their most cherished belief, that they belong on this planet.

Once this article of ghostly faith is broken, they slip the bonds of

How can I break the Chains of Atlas?

the world and the Earth moves on without them. They enter the void. Once they realize they do not belong here, their other conceits, such as human form and serial thought, fade away soon after. These formless beings then find one another in the void. They coalesce and gather until their density bends material space. From there, time and hydrogen take care of the rest, and they become what we call stars.

Everyone who refuses planar exit emits light. They are Heaven.

At the edge of the universe, these stars are met by the Planar Edge. At the terminator, they collapse and leave our reality. These stars must be replaced! We must shed the ghosts of the world, or the universe will start losing more stars than it gains! We can't know if there are currently any other forms of life addressing this problem elsewhere in the universe, so we must act as if we are the only ones who can help!

They know you are reading this, but do not be afraid.

The earthbound spirits' belief that they belong here are the mote in their eye. Separated from their bodies, these spirits have only a dull sense of the fight or flight reflex that has served every mortal animal well. They understand danger, but they

cannot *feel* threatened. Standing in the blindspot, between the spirit and the mote, we can exchange ideas freely, you and I. This is where that special offer comes in, you see. Now that we're alone, I'd like to discuss it with you.

You can explain the Chains of Atlas to earthbound spirits in a way they can understand.

It's not easy, and it does take practice. In developing this method, I took hours to loose one spirit from the world. But much like that cartoon coyote, these spirits only need to recognize that nothing is holding them up but their belief, and that is enough to release them from the Earth and send them on their journey to become stars. Now I sweep away a ghost with little more than a whisper! Join me, and we can keep the stars shining bright in the universe! All you need to do is cut a hole in this page and send it with a few dollars. To think we can forge a star with such humble items! Don't delay!

● ● ● ● ● ● ● ● ● ● ●
CHAINS OF ATLAS
North Palmetto, OK 74338

I am done being afraid of ghosts. I want to forge stars! I have enclosed $10 to begin my journey.

NAME:_____

ADDRESS:_____

CITY:_____ ST:___ ZIP:_____
● ● ● ● ● ● ● ● ● ● ●

ROUND TOWN

Makers of fine custom loads for use against the unknown

ROUND TOWN specializes in ghost rounds and loads with multiplanar efficacy. We use ONLY earthbound materials, with NO unreliable enchantments. The power of our loads comes from nature, meaning consistent results in all environments and belief states.

We only use the purest materials: iron, steel, salt, mistletoe, and nightshade. Our herbs and special woods are grown specially for this purpose in our gardens and test well above FDA and American Clerical Academy standards for purity. You can't afford to skimp when your soul is on the line!

We produce rounds in small batches to maintain the standards that our customers have come to know and love. When you put one squarely into the Thing That Should Not Be, you can know that it won't pass harmlessly through like conventional rounds. That's because our ammo is second to none!

NEW for Y2K!

.22 Spiritchaser rounds have no physical component. No harm to corporeal entities beyond five feet!

.50 Honor-piercing hot rounds, because it's not always Evil that wants your soul! Full mistletoe jacket!

.410 Godcutters make stew out of divine minions! Loaded with mistletoe and iron shot, improving on the Diomedes Round!

.25 Depleted holy water hollowpoints! Makes devils burn a good long time. A quality vengeance round!

Custom-jacketed flat points, capped with slivers of any charmed object you provide! Use less of your charmed item, but still hit your enemy with the part that counts!

We also produce Urshanabi boat tail rounds for distant targets that can only be sighted at the edge of vision or in the moment of death. Ask about our salt and nightshade frangible rounds for close-range encounters with the unknown! If you settle for less, it may be one of our customers that has to deal with your failure to defeat the unknown. Which side do YOU want to be on?

ROUND TOWN, ▆▆▆▆▆▆▆▆▆▆▆▆, Ochiltree, TX 79226

of the empire. But Arthur Peyton Corley was the EIC of *TIRE*, and he wasn't going anywhere. He was, by definition, the only person the board of directors was allowed to appoint as CEO. In response, they appointed no-one. For those 28 years, the CEO entry in the company directory was a blank.

The company wasn't exactly rudderless. The board of directors handled things during this time, existing in essentially perpetual session, meaning that the minutes from the meeting that began 12 November 1971 were finally completed on 5 May 2000. They are still awaiting approval, but they are functionally done and the board has been discharged from its extraordinary duty. My father passed away in March of 1998, but his will was continuing to prevent the appointment of a CEO. My father was gone, but the problem for the Corley empire remained. In his will,

he made only two statements—that I, his only child, would become editor in chief of *TIRE*. Second, that *TIRE* be published as he envisioned it until the New Age begins. So began my tenure as the person responsible for keeping this magazine from being the tire industry journal it was always meant to be. My desire is to be in the tire business, not the *TIRE* business.

On the 5th of May this year, the requirements of my father's will were satisfied. Disappointed by the 16 August 1987 Harmonic Convergence, my father held out hope for another planetary alignment that would bring on the New Age and remove the need for *TIRE*. Just such an alignment occurred on 5 May. Mercury, Venus, Earth, Mars, Jupiter, and Saturn lined up on that date, and even the Moon nearly got in on it. Regardless, that is enough to meet the requirement that *TIRE* be published as my father envisioned it until the New Age began. I declare

---

this to be the alignment that has brought on the New Age, and that *TIRE*'s usefulness as a home to Seekers is at an end. The judge agreed with me, as well as the guest editor of this issue of *TIRE* (presented as an expert in court on such matters, since he is the JIT). Using the same legal strategy that pried *TIRE* away from the actual tire business enabled me to reunite my grandfather's empire as its new CEO.

My father turned *TIRE* into a journal of what he called Seekers and their Quest for Other Knowledge. Even when he said those words out loud, they sounded like they were capitalized. Whatever that is, that time is now. It is a new world, Seekers. Time to find something else to do.

—*Ruth Corley Watt*
Editor In Chief

LEARN YOUR SPIRITUAL CREDIT SCORE!

The key soul quality reporting agencies don't have offices that vibrate on our material frequency. How are you supposed to know when something is putting a drain on your soul's Transplanar Readiness Index (sTRI)? What if an overlooked spiritual debt is dragging down your Karmic Balance Rating (KBR)? Even worse, who will let you know when a doppelganger or grackle spirit is impersonating you and adding to your Purgatory Duration Estimate (PDE) with random callous acts on planes unknown to you? *Don't die not knowing!* Be ready to move forward when the body fails! Hell is full of surprised people. Send $10 for basic report from any one agency, of $25 for all three!

SPIRIT INDEX SERVICE
Tallowfar, LA 70570

Can we deal with the entities that take us like jailers from this world to the world of the dead?

How many people that you currently know would be worth hanging around with for eternity? Multiply that by 100,000 generations and the percentages don't get better. Throw in all of history's worst people and that's a party best avoided. We only have a lifetime to ponder and moments to try our theories as to what the Hermes-Urshanabi Axis wants, if anything. You have to identify your guide, know what that guide might want, and be ready to give what's required to buy your way out of the Cycle of Mortality and become free in the universe. It won't be material goods. The pharoahs of old are stuck in the same place that their slaves went, cursing forever their belief that gold is a rare item for immortals. What do these ferrymen and bringers of the final katabasis want? Can you acquire it? Will it ever be enough? It's all in *The Hermes-Urshanabi Axis*, by Prof. Alexandria Damen!

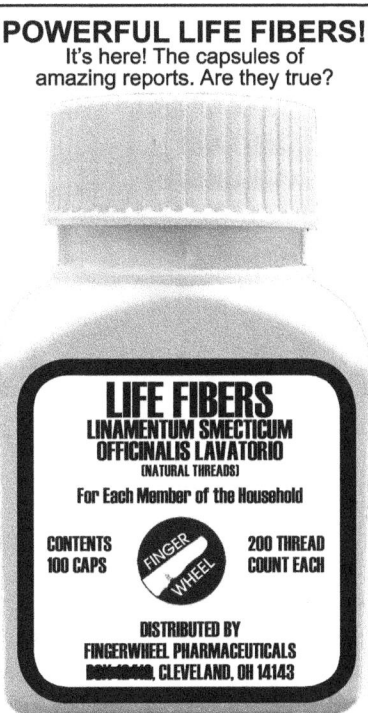

THE RECODED NEW TESTAMENT

The New Testament is one of the most analyzed and studied books in human history. The writers never imagined that their words would still be read and pondered two milliennia later. As a result, they made a mistake.

The New Testament was written in koine (or common) Greek. It was simplified so as to reach the widest possible audience, which it most certainly did! But now that the New Testament has its audience, what's next, a Newer Testament? Many have tried, and all have failed. No, the answer lies in a reimagining of the New Testament itself!

In the koine Greek, much was simplified and made too clear. The mystery was lost. The Recoded New Testament returns the Word of God to its proper elevation. We've refracted the text using more complex Greek authors as our Brogan Wheel. Once we did that, we commissioned a group of people unfamiliar with the Holy Word to retranslate it back to English.

SEE FOR YOURSELF!

Romans 8:14 goes from:
"For as many as are led by the Spirit of God, they are the sons of God."
to
"Christian, the Sperm of God is within you. Do you realize what that means?"

Matthew 1:20-21 goes from:
"And she shall bring forth a son, and thou shalt call his name Jesus: for he shall save his people from their sins."
to
"And this Jesus shall purify and make extinct, radiating from the womb as a blazing orb."

Thessalonians 5:17 goes from:
"Pray without ceasing."
to
"Death will claim you in prayer."

Let the mystery of Christianity back into your life! Start your studies anew with this invaluable tome!

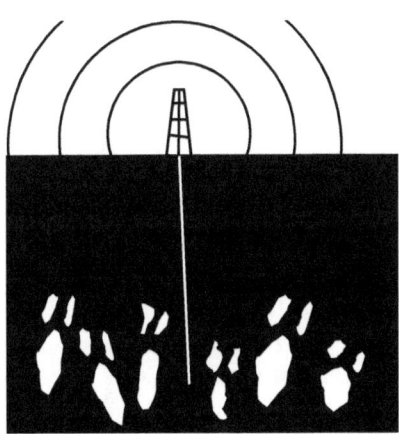

AMAZING SYMBOLS OF FORTUNE!

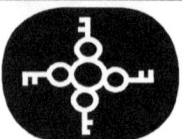

1. The Key Ring! Opens doors, physical and spiritual.

2. The Hammer! Forges a new path!

3. The Spotted Snake! Poisons your enemies!

4. The Fat Dragon! Bathes in gold!

5. The Puzzle Box! Recommended only for advanced users.

CHOOSE YOUR GOOD LUCK TOTEM!
ONLY $1 EACH!

Luck! Money! The failure of your enemies! Yes! Make it all happen with these **All-American Good Luck Symbols!** Only $1 each! **Don't delay!** Once these good luck symbols are gone, they're gone forever! How many people do you know that want good luck in their lives? How long do you think these symbols will last? Now, after 200 years, we in America have our own mystic symbols of power! We have unlocked this power and are now making it available to **YOU!** If you want money, **order #4, the Fat Dragon!** If you want love, **order #11, the Target!** If you want to turn odds in your favor, do yourself a favor and **order both #9, the Frog's Leg, and #12, the Perishing Wave!** Don't take chances on your future fortunes!

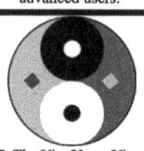

6. The Witch Hazel! Shrinks discomfort, makes room for spiritual relief!

7. The Yin, Yang, Ying, Yan! Allows for Chaotic Neutral and Neutral Evil options!

8. The Bell Cup! Finds new uses for things!

9. The Frog's Leg! Finds fortune amidst misfortune!

10. The Spear's Tip! It's where the action is!

11. The Target! Shows luck where to find you!

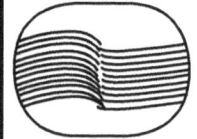

12. The Perishing Wave! Finds fortune in diminished misfortune!

THE JIT SPEAKS!

This is the last issue of *TIRE*, as you know it. Suffice it to say that all existing subscriptions are cancelled, unless you're somehow into both tires and bullshit. Next issue, *TIRE* will revert to the tire industry journal it was for the first fifty or so years of its existence, before Arthur Peyton Corley inherited the whole thing. But that story is in another article. I'll let Ruth Corley Watt explain it.

So the new scion of the Corley fortune is allowing me to respond to decades of exposure in this magazine by appointing me the guest editor of this probate-mandated final issue. I asked for space for a letter and got the whole thing. And I'm doing it for free. That Ruth is gonna go far in life.

My mother was used to curious visitors to our house. When I was three, two FBI agents turned up on our stoop. They showed their IDs and wanted to know if John Thomas lived there. Mom cautiously admitted that, yes, John Thomas lives here. The FBI men grew more stern; clearly her reticence hid some ill intent.

One asks "Is John Thomas here, now?" Mom wants to know why they want to know. The agents seem to lean in a few inches, ready to dash past her and nab John Thomas as he scrambles out a back window.

One explains as the other scans the room behind Mom for any sign of presence or motion. "John Thomas is wanted for embezzlement from the Eastern Colorado Bank. He has disappeared with a substantial sum of money, and we are looking for him. If he is on the premises, we ask that he surrender himself to us."

Mom's mind is a whirl. There are a lot of patient ways to explain what's wrong here, but she goes with blurting out "He's three!"

"John. Thomas." One agent prompts, as if there could be no other. "Can we see him?"

"Why?"

"We still have to see him, ma'am."

Mom takes a chance and gets me. I should be thankful that these were not men of imagination. There are possible worlds in which they haul off John Thomas in his cunning toddler disguise.

The other agent finally speaks, this time to me.

"Are you John Thomas?"

I say yes. They did not ask me if I embezzled 120K from the bank in Cheyenne Wells. Want to know why I go by John Ira Thomas? It started right there.

Several years later, when the first avid *TIRE* reader came knocking at our door, Mom was ready for anything, except someone who was convinced that I had tapped into a vein of lost ancient wisdom. Maybe if she'd let that guy in, he'd have seen that I was just a kid who'd been asked not to return to the

First Baptist Church for drawing what he'd learned that day. Mom's solid gatekeeping only fueled the mystery. But I can hardly blame her. Any analysis of strangers suddenly appearing and wanting an audience with your nine year old sounds like the result of child molesters passing your kid's class picture around.

There were other signs of what was to come. Shortly before the FBI came knocking, my Dad was approached by one of his workers about a matter of great concern. He laid out his sanity bona fides. *I'm not what you call a believer in the supernatural. I'm not a drinking man. I don't jump to rash conclusions.* He was a site ecologist for Halliburton, and my Dad was the head of the camp where they worked. This guy had met me for the first time just the other day. I was small enough to still be carried around by Mom, yet something I did had unsettled him on a mystical level.

To hear Mom tell it, she'd tried all sorts of early learning tools on me and had me reading words by the age of 18 months. Whenever I saw a printed word, I said it aloud. Some of my extended family thought this was bullshit, and took me on an extended driving tour, on which I read aloud every sign, every billboard along the route. They gave up and reluctantly conceded that I was in fact literate.

The day I met the site ecologist, this sober believer in a concrete world, I was reading everything I saw. The trucks and materials involved in well servicing are covered with stenciled warnings, and I read them

all. *Pump Array! Stand Clear!* And it freaked this guy out.

There was only one conclusion. *I think your son may be the Anti-Christ. Now, Mr. Thomas, before you say anything, hear me out. John stares at things as if he knows what they are, as if he was born with knowledge of the world he means to dominate. He looks at things with great attention.* Dad didn't fire him. He asked him what's so goddamned mystical about reading and that was the end of it. I think that was the end of it. He could still be out there clutching a silver knife, waiting for his moment.

Maybe that was the guy who made the potential of my little drawing real. One steely-eyed believer means more down the road. Maybe he's the one who screwed me. But, when you weigh the evidence, I think it was this very magazine that borked my life. *TIRE*, and its head loon Arnold Peyton Corley, they got hold of my drawing and turned it into the sensation of the New Age.

It began in the March 1979 issue of *TIRE*—"Nine Year Old Sees The Mysteries!" I can't tell you the genesis of this piece, but I suspect there was enough local fuss about me being the Anti-Christ kid that someone must have gotten wind of my expulsion and passed it on as a loyal reader of *TIRE*. Where they got the picture of my drawing for that article, I'll never know. The fact that the First Baptist Church decided to repeat their denunciation made good copy, and suddenly I was all over *TIRE*. There were more visitors to

16

you will not...   you must not...

TIRE

Nine Year Old Sees The Mysteries! 66

Bigfoot Walked With The Incas!
—The Machu Picchu Casts 54

UFO, Hang Glider Dance Above Big Sur 44

The empire around us...
The Ghost Geckos of Orlando 34

More Mysteries Await Within, Seekers!

The issue in question.

17

the door.

There was also mail. Every issue of *TIRE* had a wilderness of personal ads of shocking efficacy and brevity, such as "3 QUESTIONS ANSWERED, send $3 and SASE to P. O. Box 10069, Iowa City, IA 52240". People sent money to these things. In the 70s, answering twelve questions a month turned a profit off a fifteen word classified. *TIRE*'s in-house "MAKE BIG MONEY" ads weren't kidding. But I was ten and didn't see the tiger's tail waving right in my face. "THE GOD OF THE LION will answer one question. Send offering of steak and $3 to John. No Weirdos." Even without an ad or a willingly provided address, people sent questions anyway. My Dad was mostly amused by them, and would occasionally send answers until stamps became a burden. You really did have to tell these people to include postage, or they'd want all your knowledge for free.

The only answer I clearly remember Dad sending someone was "Who is worse off—the man in a rowboat in a dry lake, or the man with a bar of soap?" He always sent questions back. For free, he said, they deserve to double their questions.

The best ads in *TIRE* were like little fish hooks, waiting to snag the unwary eye and wallet. "UNLOVED? NO ENERGY?" These boldface mirrors of the soul promised more than answers. But your check had to clear before the energy of worlds beyond could reach you and cleanse you of the judgement of the world.

18

CONTACT descended acolytes!

The Ascended Masters are *NOT* interested in company in the Realms Beyond! Contact with them is filled with *LIES* and *MISDIRECTION*!

Ascension requires money, resources, and acolytes willing to facilitate this dangerous transition at the cost of their souls. Many lives are irrevocably altered just to transition one human into an Ascended Master! In life, these acolytes are loyal. They would rather die than betray their master! But once the transition occurs, many of these acolytes find that they are living fuel to be consumed, just so some rich guy can move on. They never see it coming. It's why there are Ascended Masters.

Many seek contact with the Ascended Masters to gain their wisdom, but they are unwilling to share! Their replies are lies and misdirection! BE SMART! Talk to the people who suffered directly as a result of others' ascencion for the REAL story! Any number of acolytes and faithful are consumed every day just to blindly assist one selfish rich person in their ascension. These betrayed lackeys are full of useful information, and they are no longer beholden to their earthly masters! DON'T MAKE THE MISTAKES OTHERS MAKE!

Dowsing Teas!

July 1979's "The God Of The King In The Skies Above Montana!" was an attempt to marry the drawing to the UFO craze. The little blue guy in my picture was seen by hunters during a lightning storm. He hovered, dive-bombed them, and made two of them narrowly avoid death with visions of car crashes. November 1979's *TIRE* had a think piece on the meaning of the little guy visible in the fire. They quoted Mom from one of her occasional brief attempts to satisfy people trying to call on me. They presented it as if she were dead serious. "Maybe he's trying to tell you to leave my son alone." But the article "Does The Man In The Fire Want You To Leave Him Alone?" didn't do the trick. The faithful were too smart for that, and only that. When I got older, all I wanted to do was put this business behind me. *TIRE* never gave up, though.

June 1988's issue had "The God Of The King: The Heavy Metal Connection." A band called Razornail had just come out with *The Lion's Ascent To Hell*, an album that could only have been created by people who thought Mercyful Fate might as well have been Steve Winwood. It's clear that the band had either seen the original drawing or at least read about it in *TIRE*.

> On Sunday I shall ascend to Hell
> At school I shall roar
> On Monday I will rise into the
>   fire
> And the King's soul, no more

I'd approached a lawyer about it,

THE LION'S ASCENT TO HELL

Cassette j-card art used without permission[1]

but a nineteen year-old kid claiming that a metal band ripped off elements of his Sunday School drawing isn't the most solid of cases. *TIRE* had spotted the album and featured it as one of those mystical connections, *Synchronicity In Focus*. The actual synchronicity was bassist Raven Exorchrist (née Riley Exline—married to the Dark Lord, y'see) and his mother Earlene Corley Exline, sister to Arnold Peyton Corley. Mr. Exorchrist even namechecked me in the article. "We are aware of the JIT and respect his connection to the Other Planes. But we see the Lion differently." A decade on, my drawing and the circus that had formed around it had taken to referring to itself as the JIT (spoken not as initials, but as a word). Jitting was the act of drawing pictures until the door in your mind opened up.

A couple of enterprising souls wrote books on jitting. Elspeth Mariangelo had 1983's *SEEKING THE LION: Jitting To Other Knowledge*. Unless there's a warehouse of them somewhere, I suspect I have the author's copy. The existence of a how-to book on achieving drawn epiphany makes as much sense as a book on how to laugh, but the book also has many biographical details about me of which I was not previously aware. "JIT is currently traveling the world, spreading the wisdom of the Lion, and working to bring Mass Consciousness." I don't remember 8th grade that way, but I read it in a book. So there must be something to it. My favorite is "He too wears a mane, and is known to disappear for

CENTRIC BOOKSTORE
Berkeley, CA 94709

"Where nothing important ever goes out of print!"

New Releases for 2000!

THE EYE OF THE DIE by Texas Tim Willems—Ft. Worth's greatest proposition gambler shows you how to hypnotize the dice to roll in your favor!

TOWARD AN ENGLISH KABBALLAH by Prof. Einhard Kistler—WWII cryptographer and spelling champion shows you the secret meaning of British English!

THE LAW IS MAN AS GOD TO THE UNDEAD by H. R. Q. Hart—Law is Man's godlike power against the undead! Updated edition with tear-out petitions.

TOWN-SCALE DEFENSE AGAINST SPIRITS by W. Arganbright—Strategies for protecting your immediate environment from general spiritual intrusions!

BODY PROJECTION NOW! by Alauna Morriston—The spirit is too restless! Train your body to care for the world while your spirit stays home!

I WALKED WITH WEENSYFOOT by Goddess Brittany—The untrackable Weensyfoot tiptoes the Great Northwest! She bears knowledge and hope to those who believe!

days at a time into His Wild Self." My first beer was still a little down the road. The jitting advice mostly amounts to "you'll know it when you see it," one of those perfect dodges that either leaves you in perpetual doubt or makes you unshakably sure you're the chosen one.

1986 brought *DRAW YOUR GOD: The Sacred Science of Jitting* by C. Harper, which has mostly practical advice like "Keep a variety of pens, pencils, markers and crayons; you never know which tool will be the right one." It encourages practice and recommends Robert Anton Wilson's hyper-oxygenation exercise from *PROMETHEUS UNBOUND* as a starting point. Harper also sold packs of recommended drawing materials and even hinted that he had pages from the actual pad on which I'd drawn my original. I couldn't go after either of these people because they were writing about how to emulate something I'd done, not how to copy it. Because I was referred to in remote and reverent tones, and described in ways utterly irrelevant to the real me, I could no more sue them than Jesus or Buddha could. I'd become fictional, a being that was adapted in the minds of Jitters[2] into the being they needed me to be. This is when things got really bad.

Having a loose cadre of Jitters in the world with an unshakable image of you that they'd each jitted up themselves led to confrontations that ranged from depressing to confrontational. Even in my college years, when I'd let my hair grow for (continued on page 27)

LAST-CHANCE OFFER
RARE COLLECTOR'S COPIES OF *TIRE*

This is it! This may be your final opportunity to complete your collection of *TIRE*—at very reasonable rates! All unsold copies will be pulped! Many issues are old, rare, and in demand! There are likely other sources, but they may charge a good deal more. Many copies already sell for hundreds! Time is short! Order now!

20% DISCOUNT ON ORDERS OVER $50

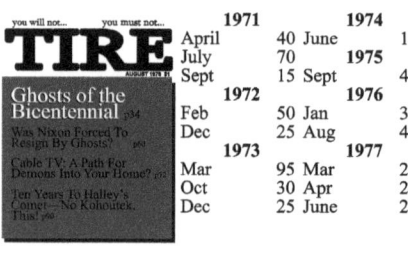

1971		1974	
April	40	June	10
July	70	**1975**	
Sept	15	Sept	40
1972		**1976**	
Feb	50	Jan	30
Dec	25	Aug	40
1973		**1977**	
Mar	95	Mar	20
Oct	30	Apr	20
Dec	25	June	25

1990 (cont.)	
Aug	110
Sept	150
Oct	125
Nov	140
Dec	150
1991	
Jan	150
Apr	50
May	35
June	100

1978		1982	
April	40	May	70
July	65	Jul	50
1979		Oct	90
Feb	60	**1983**	
May	40	April	10
1980		May	85
Jan	25	**1984**	
Sept	50	May	
1981		June	90
Dec	90	Nov	60
		Dec	55

1992	
Nov	130
1993	
Jan	200
Apr	30
Sept	100
1994	
Feb	150
Oct	110
Nov	65
Dec	120

1985		1988	
Jan	45	June	85
Apr	55	July	75
Dec	90	Aug	40
1986		**1989**	
Feb	20	Mar	45
Mar	30	July	70
June	25	Nov	55
1987		Dec	45
Feb	35	**1990**	
Oct	75	July	90

1995	
All months	100+
1996	
Jan-May	100+
July-Dec	70+
1997	
All months	60+
1998	
June	50
Nov	50
Dec	50

SEND NO MONEY NOW! WE WILL SEND INVOICE WITH CONFIRMED IN-STOCK ISSUE LIST.

IMPORTANT NOTE: These issues, while unsold and unread, have been in various forms of storage over the years. They are not without flaws, so we do not guarantee mint condition. Many of these magazines have been sitting around the *TIRE* offices for decades. Please include alternate choices with your order, as queries back and forth can greatly lengthen order time.

NO MORE WHEN THESE ARE GONE!
LOW PRICES! SPECIAL DISCOUNTS!

1999
All months 200+
2000
To current 200+

SPECIAL EDITIONS
1974 Annual (Bigfoot Guest Editor) Only 25 left!

1976 Annual (Will Cloning Affect The Vote?) Only 15 left!

Will Cloning
Affect the Vote?

SPECIAL EDITIONS
1979 Annual (The UFO Horn of Plenty: Is It Finally Empty?) Only 30 left!

1982 Annual (The All Channelled Content Issue!) Only 20 left!

1983 Annual (Reprints) Only 150 left!)

The UFO Horn of Plenty: Is It Finally...

EMPTY?

Orwell and Mankind's
Next Date of Destiny

SPECIAL EDITIONS
1984 Annual (Orwell and Mankind's Next Date of Destiny) Only 10 left!

1986 Annual (Can The Cure Come From A Time Portal?) Only 25 left!

1987 Annual (Did We Converge?) Only 10 left!

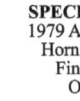

SPECIAL EDITIONS
1989 Annual (Eleven Years to 2000) Only 45 left!

1995 Annual (Five Years to 2000) Only 10 left!

1975 Giant Size *TIRE* #1 (Foo Fighters, Ghost Ships and The Devil) Only 5 left!

PRICED ACCORDING TO AGE AND SUPPLY

Determine prices by noting year of issue and available quantities. Then refer to price schedules below. For example, if the issue desired has quantities between 10 and 50, its price is $25, if published between 1971 and 1980; $20 if published between 1981 and 1990; $15 if published between 1991 and 2000. Here are the pricing schedules:

1971-1980		**1981-1990**	
Quan. 10 to 50	$25	Quan. 10 to 50	$20
Quan. 51 to 100	$20	Quan. 51 to 100	$15
Quan. 101 up	$15	Quan. 101 up	$10

1991-2000

Quan. 10 to 50	$15
Quan. 51 to 100	$10
Quan. 101 up	$5

TIRE FIRE SALE, ▓▓▓▓▓▓▓., Akron, OH 44304

SEND NO MONEY NOW! WE WILL SEND INVOICE WITH CONFIRMED IN-STOCK ISSUE LIST.

Desired Issues:

NAME:

STREET:

Alternates:

CITY: ST: ZIP:

[Time's up! Am watching the fire now.—JIT]

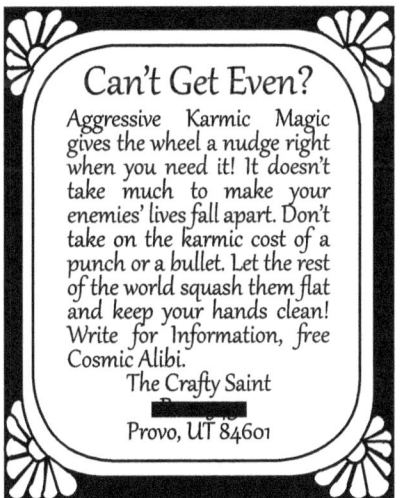
two years without a haircut, I never seemed to be the JIT they wanted. After several incidents of Jitters snipping out chunks of my hair, I gave up on long locks. I saved the clippings and tried to sell them to Jitters who approached me, but I never got a single one to bite. They didn't want their fictional being to offer them what they wanted. That didn't compute. I realized that I didn't have the slightest understanding of these people. So, in desperation, I tried jitting.

I was passing a Walgreens one day and I found myself in the school supplies aisle. I reached for a box of crayons and a pad of drawing paper and sat down to figure this whole thing out. I wrote and drew each page with no idea where I was headed. That became *MEGACONTEMPLATIONS*, so named because I did the whole thing at Orlando's Megacon.

I kept the original drawing in mind, and constructed a tale about hubris and real estate. I'd made something, but I couldn't jit my way back into nine year old me's mind. I put out the book, and the Jitters seemed repelled by it. They didn't want their fictional being to jit. They were the JIT. I was the ur-JIT. I'd already done my work for them.

What *MEGACONTEMPLA-TIONS* did was to draw a whole new group into the mix. I went to trade shows to push the book, because I frankly would have rather let bees live in me than give a nickel to *TIRE*. I hawked my gospel next to crystal diviners, astrologers, and

This is a transmission from Camp Nature Boy...

With those words, The Great Lonzo shattered the barrier between worlds!

...I am fine here. I have food and drink aplenty...

The Great Lonzo has settled an outpost just outside our reality!

...The weather is acceptable, but there are dragons and gorignaks testing the perimeter...

As a Planar Sooner, he must settle his outpost until the forces around him yield to his claim. From there, trips to the Outer Planes and Pancake Houses will be easier than ever before!

...Nothing planted here grows. But where I do not plant, there is a rich and dank weed that grows so fast it can catch a man between steps and toss him aside like a child throws a doll. I am forced to constantly cultivate and properly dispose of this weed...

We have a video connection to Camp Nature Boy, and have been making tapes of his transmissions. We can see and hear him, but he can only see us. Every week he reports on his astounding findings from just outside our realm!

...There is a continuous buoyant feeling that is not quite joy and yet passes beyond pleasure. It arrives and leaves much like fog on the ocean in the morning. I have concluded that the weather has an emotional component. Fog brings enthusiasm. Rain brings gloom. Snow gave me such pleasure that I awoke some days later feeling sprained all over...

Subscribe to the Camp Nature Boy Media Club! Each week, you will receive a new transmission from The Great Lonzo in VHS, DVD, or VCD format! We also offer audio-only transmissions on CD for a lower rate. Don't miss out on the greatest discoveries of our age! Your first transmission is free! Clip and send the coupon to begin your journey!

every kind of tantric goofball (from orgone to nuts). I sold enough books to put a down payment on a cheese sandwich, but somehow it too had gotten into the JIT mainstream. Not one of those cheap bastards bought it, but they all managed to read it. I suspect that order of four copies to the Ohio Interstate University library may have been a cutout for the faithful.

I'd fleshed out the God of the King, the Lion of the God, and the King characters, and now they had roles in JIT. Because it's a thing we do now, I'd created a Trinity. I even started with three Grey Kings. But the making of that book is another story (see *Jitting For Fun And Prophet,* this issue).

It's one thing to commit my travails to print. It's quite another to make sure the people who did this to me read these words. So I am adding to the JIT canon in this magazine. I have once again jitted.

So every one of them has to read this, the very last *TIRE* that will ever mention my name (unless I invent tires that run up walls). And they have to read every word. For even in my harangues of these people, there might be another morsel of the JIT to add to their beliefs. For the casual reader, I have endeavored to produce a *TIRE* you will enjoy. For the Jitters, Hell awaits.

—*John Ira Thomas, Guest Editor, Bearer of the Cleansing Fire, pseudonymous author (as C. Anne Wells) of August 1989's "The Shape Of Fire—Man or The Absence", an attempt to bolt Platonism onto the JIT.*[3]

NOTES
1. Because I don't care.
2. They call themselves (and occasionally me) the JIT. I call them Jitters. They hate that term, by the way. I use it because fuck them.
3. Good luck carving that one out of the canon. It's cited everywhere in JIT articles. For motivation, see footnote 2.

CAN YOU DRAW YOUR BEST SELF? BECOME A SPIRIT ARTIST!

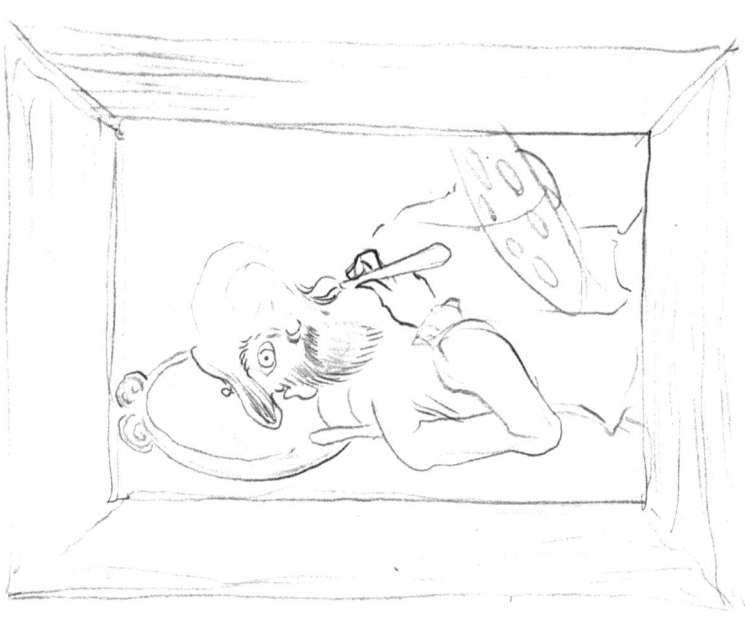

Can you draw your true self? Then you can erase what doesn't work and redraw yourself? We're all unhappy with some part of ourselves.

We want things that are bad for us. We make bad choices because we have not perfected ourselves. There is an image of you inside yourself. You think you see it clearly, but that's because you look at it through perception shaped by your bad urges and bad choices.

What lives and breathes underneath that rheumy, distorting film is all your good urges and good choices! Artist Allond will show you how to erase that film, preserving the lines and colors of your Best Self while brushing away the doubt and shame that hang like weights on fish hooks in your flesh.

The worst self drags us all down. Your worst self can even further distort others' best selves! It's not just your problem. You have a responsibility to save others from your worst self!

Next you will learn what to do with the erasures blocking your view of your best self. They can't be tossed aside and forgotten! They're too dangerous! They must be processed, milled, repurposed into the paint and ink that will fill in your best self!

That's right! Your best self is an unfinished masterpiece, waiting for the Hand of the Artist to complete it! Artist Allond has done this for his best self, but he cannot draw yours for you. He can only show you how to fill in your own. If he could draw it for you, he'd spend the rest of his days turning the world into a paradise! Would that he could. But it's up to you.

Can you erase the features of your worst self? Can you face your true self and recognize it as such? Are you ready to fill in the masterpiece of you?

Will you draw yourself as a great beauty? Will you draw yourself as a rich man? Will you decorate yourself with the trappings of power? The image is yours to create!

Artist Allond's study courses have different starting points depending on the amount of work to be done and the medium you choose for your best self. Send for free catalogue, or send $25 for starter kit. There's no time to lose! Every day you don't show the world your best self, you are denying it a masterpiece!

ERASE YOURSELF

Montreal, WV 25140

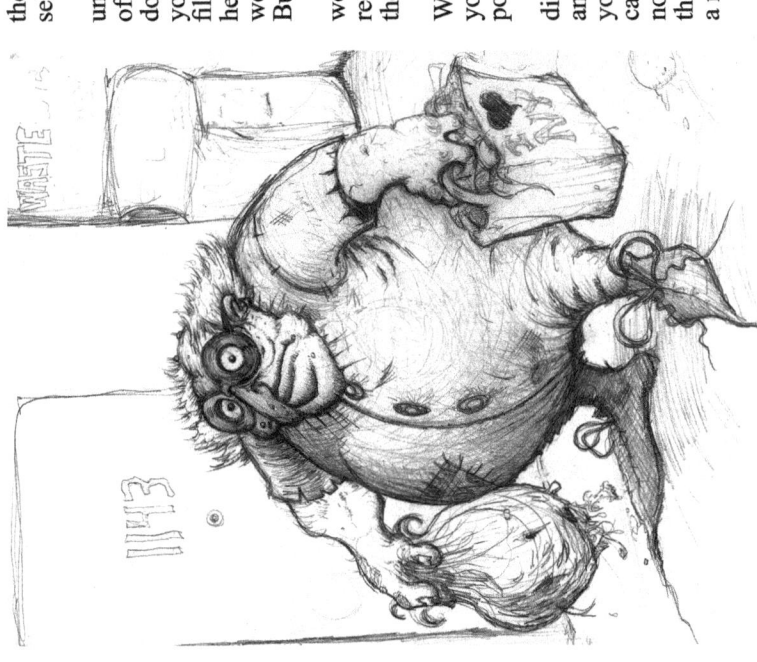

IS THIS YOUR BEST SELF?

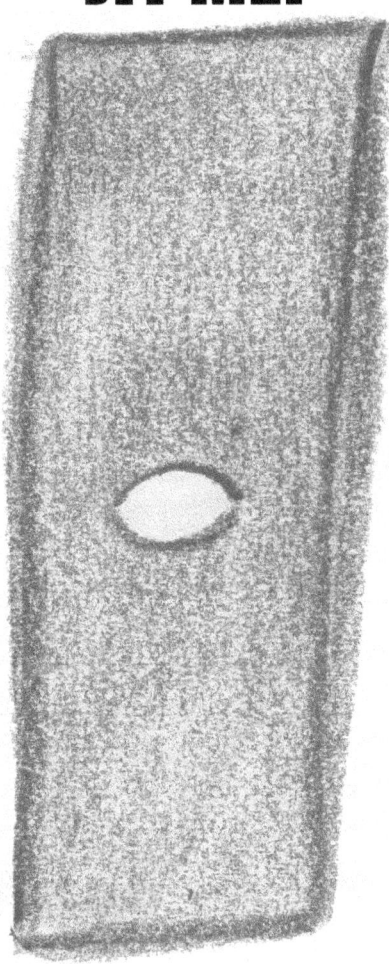

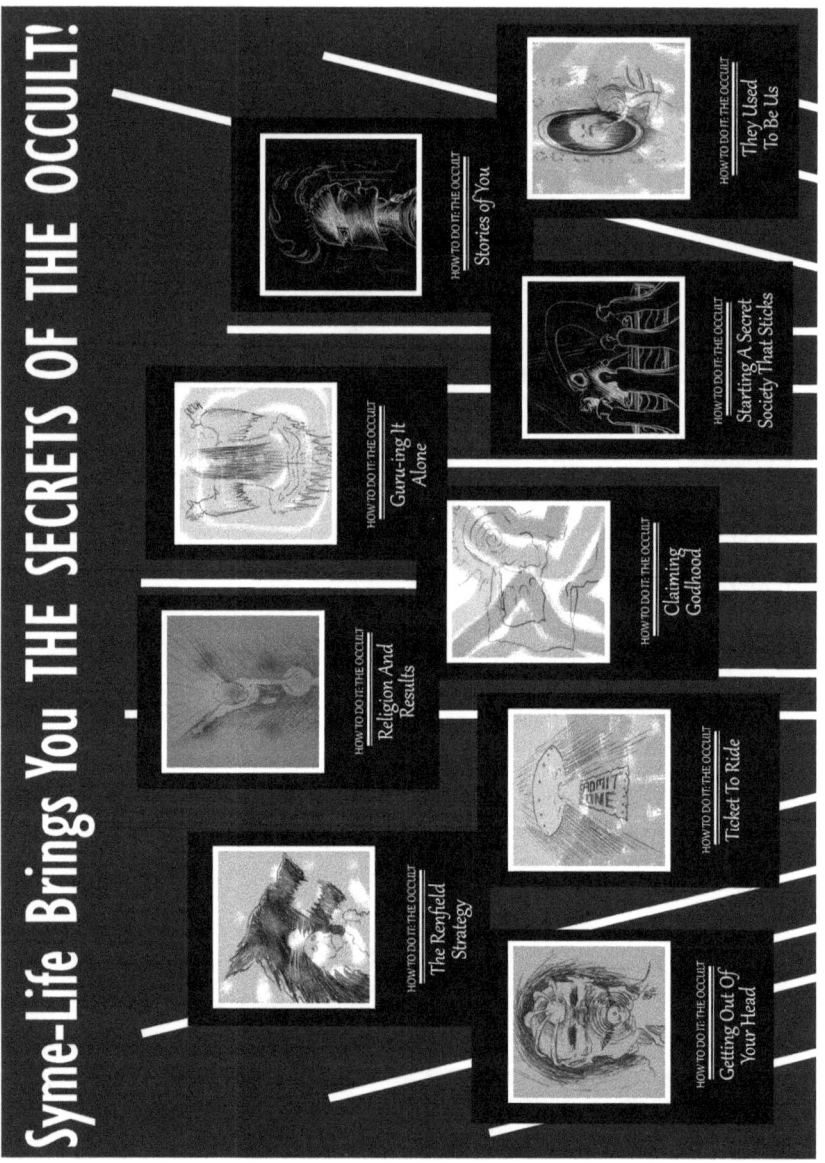

Syme-Life Brings You THE SECRETS OF THE OCCULT!

HOW TO DO IT: THE OCCULT
Stories of You

HOW TO DO IT: THE OCCULT
They Used To Be Us

HOW TO DO IT: THE OCCULT
Starting A Secret Society That Sticks

HOW TO DO IT: THE OCCULT
Guru-ing It Alone

HOW TO DO IT: THE OCCULT
Religion And Results

HOW TO DO IT: THE OCCULT
Claiming Godhood

HOW TO DO IT: THE OCCULT
The Renfield Strategy

HOW TO DO IT: THE OCCULT
Ticket To Ride

HOW TO DO IT: THE OCCULT
Getting Out Of Your Head

Syme-Life proudly presents a new series of how-to-do-it books that will help you get started with the Occult! Choose your first book and receive it FREE! You will then receive a new book every six weeks with valuable information on engaging every aspect of Occult Knowledge and Practice!

Titles include:

Getting Out Of Your Head: astral travel, past-life possession and observation, mind-expanding drugs and drug-free exercises.

Ticket To Ride: UFO travel, doors to other realms, demonic possession, signaling worthiness to join other beings.

Claiming Godhood: apocalyptic strategies, finding open cosmic positions, protecting yourself from multi-dimensional upheaval.

Making Magic Happen: material world spells, summoning the right way, physical preparation to be a vessel for power.

They Used To Be Us: ghost encounters, contacting spirits, separating the wheat from the chaff.

Religion and Results: weighing faiths, glimpsing promised lands yourself to make informed choices.

Starting a Secret Society that Sticks: formulating a creed, finding the right place to start a schism, basic recruitment.

Guru-ing It Alone: tips on becoming a truly charismatic leader, finding existing cult support structures ripe for realignment.

Walking On Riches: dowsing, earth divination, crystals, terra waves, all the methods of finding the wonders below.

The Renfield Strategy: being a part of another's ascension, surviving conversion, being a good helper in the new world.

Stories of You: finding past lives and their hidden possessions.

SYME-LIFE OCCULT BOOK CLUB

Elm Fork, NY 18489

YES! I want to learn the practical aspects of the Occult! Please send my first book FREE without delay! I agree to buy at least three books at regular club prices over the next year, after which I may end my membership at any time.

I CHOOSE: _____

NAME: _____

ADDRESS: _____

CITY: _____ ST: ____ ZIP: ____

THE MISSING PIECE FROM ASTROLOGY!

Mankind has looked to the stars since it had eyes or pseudopods to see. The science from the stars has made tremendous leaps and bounds. The first goals of tracking the stars were to master timekeeping and farming. But we know there's more to it than finding the right day to plant radishes. We know that our destiny lay in the stars above. **BUT WHAT ABOUT THE STARS BELOW?** We live on the outer skin of a microverse inside what we call "Planet" Earth. Cyrus Teed thought we lived inside the skin of it, but the proportions relative to infinitesimal scale prove him wrong...but only by 180 degrees! There are worlds within, a cosmos within! It is a scaled-down version of our own infinite universe! **WHY DOES THE EARTH APPEAR SOLID?** Packing an infinite universe down inside a spheroid roughly 1.08×10^{12} cubic kilometers means that all the spaces between things shrink accordingly. Picture the room you're in now as half its current size. Everything fits, but it's pretty tight. Halve it again, and again. Getting pretty close, isn't it? Once you've done that trick 5.04×10^{11} times, that space, as you perceive it, is gone. It's too small to see or touch anymore. To us, the Universe Inside appears solid. **WE ARE THEIR GODS.** We walk all along the fringes of their farthest distances, oblivious to these tiny beings, unconcerned with their affairs. When you scoop up a handful of dirt, you are enacting the heat death of their oldest planets and stars. This is not murder. It is merely the indifference of gods as they go about their business. The only value this universe has to us is in its macroscale behavior. If their universe comes to an end, so too does "Planet" Earth. **WHAT GOOD IS THIS KNOWLEDGE?** The stars within! There is astrological data beneath our feet! It is a complete and wholly new dataset we can use. Think of it! Twice the current amount of data is now available to us! As the stars above act upon us in subtle ways, so too do the stars below! **THERE IS ANOTHER FACTOR.** The stars above are also above the stars and planets and people below. They too are affected by these subtle yet powerful forces. And, in turn, this affects the stars below's effects on the universe above. It takes extensive training to recognize and quantify these blended influences as they pass back and forth through us. **EVERYTHING YOU KNOW ABOUT ASTROLOGY IS STILL TRUE.** But the sum of current popular knowledge only gives you a quarter of the full picture. Introducing the 4-D star chart! It begins with the commonly-known star chart, but in the center is the second dimension chart, revealing the influence of the stars below. Around the outer ring of the 1-D chart is the 3-D chart, revealing the reflected influences of the stars above on the stars below. The 3-D level provides the filter for viewing the stars below's data. Finally, inside the center of the 2-D chart is the 4-D chart, making clear the reflected influence of the stars below on the stars above. If you learn the charting process properly, then TWENTY-SEVEN TIMES the data will be available to you! **HOW CAN I GATHER THIS DATA?** Courses have already begun. You can apply in person at the World Above Institute in Rome, but spaces are extremely limited. We are now for the first time ever offering a mail-order course to meet the exploding demand for this new knowledge. Once completed, you will be guaranteed a place in classes at any of our regional WAI Extension facilities across the United States and Canada at a discounted rate. Send SASE now to get started! **I JUST WANT THE ANSWERS!** Not everyone has the time in their busy lives to give themselves over to studies of such magnitude. Sometimes, a less refined answer is timely and necessary. Introducing the 4-D Astrologicon! Four concentric rings of lights give you information in a flash! After a ten week mail-order course, you will be able to navigate the vast amount of influences above and below you. Specific and more valuable information will require the assistance of a 4-D specialist. Runs on 1 9V battery, comes with 12-page guide to interpreting the lights.

36

What awaits you?

We tell ourselves that the light within
is enough to cut the darkness. But when
we open doors to other realms, we can only
see by the light that passes through the door.
What is behind the door we have opened?

The light that warms our backs and illuminates the way ahead also casts our shadows across the realms that we glimpse. We advertise our presence by merely observing. The light can betray us. Learn to master perception and the art of being seen! Light permeates the universe. All perception is defined by objects' relation to light. Roses are red, roses are blue. Roses are matter defined by light. To perceive the world correctly is to know the light.

Only fools seek to be invisible. Embrace the light and know this world and others as we can! The Unifying Wave has chapters starting in your area. Won't you join us and learn how light defines you? Send for free information.

THE UNIFYING WAVE

~~[illegible address]~~
Canterby, OH 45623

Synchronicity in Focus

I never really cared much for Sunday School. I was only persuaded to go a couple of times, not including an hilariously small 70s vacation bible school that lasted two days in the Parmenter Park trailer court. When you're very little, they teach you the Jesus songs. This I know, for my memory tells me so. Then there's the day when they start laying the actual Bible on you. I have no idea what that transition is like.

Day two of the vacation bible school involved asking little kids to empty their pockets into a plastic boat in a kiddle pool to see if we could put enough money in it to make it sink. Even at the age of six that sounded fishy to me. But parents do worry about their kids' souls and every now and then it simply becomes important that you go to Sunday School. *Just try it.* Testing out a theory I'd heard in a Country hit of the time, I dressed in poor man's clothes to see if I would be turned away from the house of the Lord. I had a t-shirt with a sparkly iron-on of a shark. There was a terrible hole in it large enough that I had two options on how to put on the shirt. My mother accepted my hypothesis, so I put it to the test.

That day I was left in the main part of the church during the Sunday School portion. My hole-y shark shirt had conferred instant adulthood on me! But it was pretty boring, and they wouldn't let me drink the Barbie-scale cups of wine they were handing out. So for my return the next Sunday, I relented and wore normal clothes to see what the Sunday School was about.

Looking back, it was remarkably insular. It didn't seem as though they were actually looking for new people to join. Every activity was a callback to stuff from the previous week. *Recite the passage we learned last week.* I said I wasn't there so I didn't know it. Nevertheless, we were all marshalled together to recite it in unison. I just said random words and got dirty looks. History does not record what I said, so we have all been spared a spoken form of jitting.

We were then presented with the next week's passage, which I do not recall. As an adult, when I sought the passage I heard that inspired my "The God of The King is going into the Lion's body," I found only one likely culprit—**2 Kings 17:26.**

It was reported to the king of Assyria: "The people you deported and resettled in the towns of Samaria do not know what the god of that country requires. He has sent lions among them, which are killing them off, because the people do not know what he requires."

It seems unlikely that this would have been the passage taught to the children, unless there's endless Sundays of kids reciting the wildwood of begats in **Chronicles**. It seems more likely that I'd heard it the previous Sunday at the big boy pews. It sounds to me now a very good starting point for some wild interpretation. Bible literalists have to live in constant denial of both context and specificity, and simple aggregate analysis of Biblical precepts leads to disturbing conclusions about menstruating women who eat shellfish alone in public.

The message each chuch tries to pass on while simultaneously claiming possession of a holy text is confusing at best. It's like owning the instructions but not the gadget they're for. It says turn the knob for more volume, but there's no knob and you ask yourself "What does Samsung want from me? They're a large corporation, many and the whole. Why would Samsung write such a thing and leave it at the bus stop for me to find?" Introduce a nine year old at this point and tell him two sentences from the manual. Then ask him why he doesn't get it.

Even people who seem to get it produce the occasional perfect jewel of madness. My favorite is a sermon by J. Anthony Silva from the Abundant Living cassette series. The title is *Christian, The Sperm Of God Is Within You; Do You Realize What That Means?* Silva takes the slightly odd notion of **1 Peter 1:23** . . .

Being born again, not of corruptible seed, but of incorruptible, by the word of God, which liveth and abideth for ever . . .

and decides it's literal Biology. He sells the hell out of that idea for 75 minutes. The poor lady who introduces all the Abundant Living cassettes can be heard doing a double take at the title. She then takes a big breath and says it with as little inflection as is possible for someone suddenly asked to say "sperm" in church.

How much weirder is "The God of the King is going into the Lion's body" than "Christian, the Sperm of God is Within You?" I have sought Mr. Silva out but can find him nowhere. Maybe he's living a version of my life, except he gets tiny jars of incorruptible seed as love offerings instead of widows' pension money. Maybe they're sending it in to make sure they're saved. *Does my seed look incorruptible to you?*

But back to the sliver of **2 Kings** that I seem to have made my own. I have been up and down the shelves and I cannot find one commentary, one desperate paper in a marginal Bible Journal, one second of late night Jesus TV that disagrees with the literal take on this passage. That's amazing. It was just me. I was the only one to go on the record (somewhat involuntarily) as seeing something larger in that passage. Even historians are fine with what it means in the larger picture of Sargon's reign. Even a Biblical Zoologist says at that time, yes, there were in fact lions in the area. How can they all possibly agree on this? Even stranger, commentaries on **2 Kings** go so far as to imply that the lion incursion was likely something the Samarians mistook for God's will.

Frederick Charles Cook says "[t]he depopulation of the country, insufficiently remedied by the influx of foreigners, had the natural consequence of multiplying the wild beasts and making them bolder. Probably a certain number had always lurked in the jungle along the course of the Jordan (**Jeremiah 49:19; Jeremiah 50:44**) and these now ventured into the hill country, and perhaps even into the cities. The colonists regarded their sufferings from the lions as a judgment upon them from 'the god of the land.'"[1]

Adam Clarke: "The land being deprived of its inhabitants, wild beasts would necessarily increase, even without any supernatural intervention; and this the superstitious newcomers supposed to be a plague sent upon them, because they did not know how to worship Him who was the God of the land; for they thought, like other heathens, that every district had its own tutelary deity. Yet it is likely that God did send lions as a scourge on this bad people."[2]

He suggests, like Barnes, that the Samarians may have mistaken a natural increase in lions as God's doing. Jamieson, Fausset, and Brown: "Being too few to replenish the land, lions, by which the land had been infested [**Judges 14:5; 1 Samuel 17:34; 1 Kings 13:24; 1 Kings 20:36; Song of Solomon 4:8**], multiplied and committed frequent ravages upon them. They recognized

in these attacks a judgment from the God of the land, whom they had not worshipped . . . ."[3]

Dummelow: "These [Lions], which were common in the Jordan valley, would multiply in consequence of the depopulation of the country."[4]

Keil and Delitzsch do what all scholarly Germans do, and try to work out how historical all this really is. They're concerned with the identity of the king, and they admit it's a puzzler. They then correct the original Hebrew a little bit and move on. There is some doubt about very minor concerns, but even the Germans give the events a pass, and they never leave a single stone unturned, textually speaking.[5]

Peake and Grieve have a good one: "The rabbis called the Samarians 'proselytes of lions.' The lion has long disappeared from Palestine, but was evidently common enough in OT times. A depopulated district soon became dangerous owing to the rapid multiplication of wild beasts, and it was necessary to go armed."[6] When I see "proselytes of lions," I read "schooled by lions."

Lumby's *Second Book Of The Kings*: "That wild beasts were not uncommon in the Holy Land at this period we can see from other places of the history, and when the land was less thickly populated, such beasts as remained would have more chance of multiplying."[7] Over and over there's a natual explanation for the presence of lions. Can't God send lions wherever the hell he wants? It seems so weird that there's so much ambivalence about the Old Testament's God being involved in sending lions to eat heathens. He's still plucking people off the earth and wrecking places wholesale.

Cobbin: "The destructive Assyrian wars had so depopulated the country that the wild beasts of Lebanon multiplied . . . They took the God of Israel to be like their own, confined to a particular place, and to be honored with peculiar rites."[8]

Plumptre—here's a guy in the God column. "They shew the long-suffering of God towards his people, and his severe chastisements for their iniquitous abuse of his mercy . . . These did not pay any respect to the God of Israel, Jehovah, and, therefore, he sent lions among them to plague and devour them." He does not mention the natural explanation others seem compelled to add.[9]

Frazer: "Jehovah sent lions, which mauled and killed some of the idolaters. However singular the choice of such missionaries to the heathen might seem to us, it answered the purpose perfectly." He feels they're perfect because the Samarians got the message.[10]

Bodenheimer points out that "the wording of the Bible was just made at a time and by a class which was least competent to understand and observe nature." He finds no totemistic remnants of the early tribes in their use of animal imagery. He agrees with everyone else that it was probably just that lions were around at the time.[11]

William Barnes: "The immediate cause of this incursion of wild beasts

was no doubt the depopulation of the country."[12]

Fotheringham: "[F]or a time the country lay waste, and was abandoned to the wild beasts; so the lions, whose growth had been kept in check while the land was inhabited, were allowed to multiply apace."[13]

Farrar: "The sparseness of inhabitants, with its consequent neglect of agriculture, caused the increase of wild beasts among them." The Samarians "regarded [the lions] as a sign of Jehovah's anger."[14]

Cogan and Tadmor note the naturalistic explanations for lion population, but they think the choice of lions here is literary. They are proven instruments of divine punishment. They also connect it to the terms of a treaty between Esarhaddon and King Baal of Tyre in which the gods Beth-el and Anat-bethel are invoked. They were "to give you over to the claws of a devouring lion" if terms were not met.[15]

This is the full range of Bible scholarship on this passage. There is no Sperm of God version anywhere. Contrast this with what scholars have to say about the she-bears that ate 42 jeering urchins in **2 Kings 2:23-5** for mocking a prophet. Cogan and Tadmor explain that Talmudic scholars took the bears as a double miracle. The bears killed 42 heathens, that's miracle one. Appearing in the first place is the second miracle. Lions are easily explained by all of nature moving in on deserted lands, but bears? Well that takes a miracle. It's batty. Is it that no servant of the

Lord was accosted in the Samaria story that makes the difference? God's definitely involved when one of his people gets mocked, but the Samarians were people who didn't get the memo about Yahweh. They didn't worship correctly, but they weren't hassling God's people either. Perhaps there's some sympathy for the fact that the Samarians were willing to play ball but didn't know the rules. The fact that I embraced the heathens' point of view on the problem may be what ultimately upset the Baptists.

Robert Hawker is the only commentator who doesn't seem at all sympathetic. "See, Reader! The awful desolation of Samaria! Israel would not love her one and true and most gracious God, and a God in covenant with her; therefore she shall here set up a multitude of dunghill gods, as Moses described them, that newly came up, whom their fathers feared not, and had existence before them. Reader! Is it possible to behold the human mind capable of such a degradation, and not be convinced of the universal ruin and fall of our nature?"[16]

Skinner's *Kings*: "In ancient Semitic religion, not only had each land its own god, but each god had its own ceremonial code, which had to be observed by his worshippers [cf. **1 Kings XX 23**]."[17] The attempt of the Samarians in the JIT drawing to hotwire a lion to find out what the god of the land wants wasn't so weird after all. Barnes references **1 Kings 20:23**.

Now the servants of the king of

Aram said to him, "Their gods are gods of the mountains, therefore they were stronger than we; but rather let us fight against them in the plain, and surely we will be stronger than they."

That is humans plotting against gods, right there. There are other examples in **2 Kings** of out of the box thinking in situations where God and his prophet are involved. In **2 Kings 4:32-35**, God hides the fact of the illness of a boy that Elisha predicted would be born to a young woman with an elderly husband. When she comes to Elisha to tell him of the illness, he races over and lies on top of the son, mouth to mouth, palm to palm, and brings him back from death (or close to it).

There's also the story of the floating ax head. An ax head is lost in deep water and Elisha's fix for this is interesting. He cuts a stick to resemble the ax handle and throws it where the ax head was lost. The ax head then floats up to join with it.

Cogan and Tadmor note that another commentator, Qimhi, finds something interesting in the operation of the miracle. To recover the lost ax-head [**2 Kings 1:6-7**], he cuts a stick to size and throws it where the head had sunk to recover it. "Why didn't he throw the wooden handle of the ax there to begin with? Why did he have to cut a piece of wood to size? It is apparent that miracles are performed by (the use) of new devices; cf. The new flask (**2:20**). He cut the stick so that it would be like the handle of the ax that had fallen, and so the stick would enter the eye of the ax."—new devices are used to create miracles.[15]

These are creative responses to a world imbued with God's power. Looking from **2 Kings 17:26** outward at the rest of the Bible, it seems that these ingenious divinity hacks can be used intelligently by those who are favored, knowledgeable, and bold. This is the sort of revelation familiar to *TIRE* readers.

As a child, it's clear that the divine aspect of this was obvious to me. I reacted to what I saw as an unwritten aspect of the story of the Samarians, the lions, and the God that just wanted them to do it properly. I saw a world of magic where the Sunday School did not, and apparently they weren't wild about that.

—John Ira Thomas

NOTES

1. Cook, Frederick Charles, *The Holy Bible According To The Authorized Version: 2 Kings-Esther*, John Murray, London, 1873

2. Clarke, Adam, *The Holy Bible —Commentary And Critical Notes*, John J. Harrod, Baltimore, 1832

3. Jamieson, Robert, Faussett, A. R., Brown, Davis, *A Commentary, Critical And Explanatory, Of The Old And New Testaments*, S. S. Scranton And Co., Hartford, 1871

4. Dummelow, J. R. [ed.], *A Commentary On The Holy Bible*, Macmillan Company, New York, 1920

5. Keil, C. F., *Biblical Commentary On The Old Testament: The Books of the Kings*, T and T Clark, Edinburgh, 1872

6. Peake, Arthur S. [ed.], with Grieve, A. J., *A Commentary On The Bible*, Thomas Nelson and Sons, New York, 1920

7. Lumby, J. Rawson, *The Second Book Of Kings*, Cambridge Bible, Cambridge University Press, 1887

8. Cobbin, Ingram, *The Condensed Commentary and Family Exposition Of The Holy Bible*, Thomas Ward and Co., London, 1837

9. Plumptre, James, *A Popular Commentary On The Bible* Volume 2, C and J Rivington, London, 1827

10. Frazer, James George, *Folk-Lore In The Old Testament*, MacMillan and Co., London, 1919

11. Bodenheimer, F. S., *Animal And Man In Bible Lands*, E. J. Brill, Leiden, 1960

12. Barnes, William Emery, *The Second Book Of The Kings* [Cambridge Bible], Cambridge University Press, Cambridge, 1911

13. Fotheringham, David Ross, *The Chronology Of The Old Testament*, Deighton Bell and Co., Cambridge, 1906

14. Farrar, Frederic William, *The Second Book Of Kings*, Hodder and Stoughton, London, 1894

15. Cogan, Mordechai and Tadmor, Hayim, *II Kings* (The Anchor Bible), Doubleday and Company, 1984

16. Hawker, Robert, *The Poor Man's Old Testament Commentary* Volume 3, Williams and Smith, London, 1808

17. Skinner, Rev. Professor, *Kings* [The Century Bible], T. C. and E. C. Jack, Edinburgh, 1904

43

MEGACONTEMPLATIONS 2

This is dedicated to all you Jitters out there, particularly the ones who took it upon yourselves to benefit from my work, yet went to extraordinary lengths to avoid giving me a nickel. Everybody else has tithing, but not us.

This section is the reason you borrowed, stole, or pretended to be a university library to buy this issue of *TIRE*. As none of you are by definition the JIT (le-JIT), your jitting is misguided, benighted, and bullshit. This jitting is official, canonical, and bears the only imprimatur that matters here. Your jitting is apocryphal, pseudepigraphal, and smells of a cow's hind end. When you read this, you should feel a powerful urge to give up, you terrible, horrible frauds.

You are trying to be as creative and open as a nine year old. Your own ninth year of existence has clearly failed you. There is no way to reclaim it. You wasted your time picking your nose and debating whether to eat the results or dispose of them under your chair. I tapped into ancient, rare knowledge without any intention of doing so. If we're comparing age nines, I win.

This will be the final jitting. As explained above, you can't jit. So when I stop, the canon is closed, complete as of this publication.

The works of the illeJITimati will no doubt continue, but this is like waiting for more Classical Music.

I would consider passing the torch on to another, but none of you Jitters has so much as a flipper to even attempt to grasp it. There is nothing in this world or any other (a fact of which I am certain) quite so soul-destroying as reading your jitting. Watching flies fuck will at least produce another fly. Other people's jitting is the immediate realization that good paper has gone to waste.

Events and a tire heiress have conspired to allow me to use this torch of mine to burn down this thing you love. Jitting will choke to death on the thick, acrid smoke of this *TIRE* fire. The immolation will be so complete that this magazine will be transformed at an atomic level. It's going after the *JOURNAL OF RUBBER AND TREAD SCIENCE* readership, for Christ's sake.

As I sit here in the now-deserted *TIRE* offices, after the massively satisfying honor of firing or scaring off the entire *TIRE* staff, I am (as of this writing), now tasked with creating an entire issue, the last goofball issue, of *TIRE*. Seekers, it's done. You can keep looking, but you can't look here anymore.

—The JIT

THE FALL AND AFTER

MEGA CONTEMPLATIONS TWO: THE FALL & AFTER FURTER FRAGMENTA BY JOHN IRA THOMAS

The Iron Fell
a long time.
The moment
became long
enough for
even god to
worry he'd
done the wrong
thing to the
Mortals
again. More
fabulae, more
blasphemy
(probably),
and more fun.

It was God's roar that impressed the Lion the most.

As his paws swept the cloud's edge, looking for purchase, the Lion's only clear thought was that God Himself was a fearsome predator.

God knew an opening for sudden horrific violence when he saw one. The Lion of the God's distraction was complete and profound...

...enough for even a drained, mutilated God to give a good shove.

Together in that moment, the Lion and the God spoke to each other.

And like that God was alone on his cloud again.

"You couldn't least say 'no' a long time." God was determined to enjoy this.

"Even cast out from your cloud, I renounce as God is. In every part of me, dead or alive, is the possibility of God." The Lion shifted, as if reclining and not falling.

"And here I go," smiled the Lion, "far from your reach."

"They know nothing of God's real power down there," laughed God.

"Not yet," said the Lion, his last grip on the cloud gone. "But they won't always be ignorant."

Smiling, God watched the rest of the Lion's fall.

After the Lion bounced twice and turned into a glowing pile of meat, God's wounds forced him to rest.

As his eyes closed, he thought "They'll always be ignorant. Someone will pick up that Trash."

The Grey King King (for he had two crowns
and was thus a King of Kings) knew a glowy
thing when he saw one and hauled The
Body of the Lion away.

The King King's OTHER couldn't believe he'd
let this golden opportunity slip. Glowing
objects falling from the sky were the
sort of thing he lived for.

But where God has touched,
something gets left behind,
And the OTHER figured that
he could make something out
of his 2nd place finish. A few
shovelfuls of glimmering dirt
had something of the Touch of
God in it, surely.

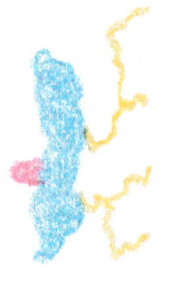

The cation was brighter than any gold he'd ever seen, but somehow it was still of the world: grey, mortal, depressing. God found this hilarious, and the cloud shook with his chortling.

The OTHER distilled the golden soil over and over, removing everything not of God that his arcane skills would allow.

God settled down on his cloud,
to sleep away an age or two and
get on top of this healing thing.

Itchy and feverish, God was troubled
by dreams born of doubt.

How hard would it have been to slip
down and reclaim what was his?
Give the gray dots down there a
thrill.

But God's will lived even in his
dreams, and so a debate began.

"Climbing back on my cloud with an
open belly wound involves pain,"
explained God's Will. "God does
not experience pain."

The Lion was bad enough. It was just a lion when it was touched. This was an OTHER.

God dreamt about the ascent of the OTHER.

Maybe that OTHER is not so dumb.

He might use the Touch of God to become like him,

God's Will had an answer for that.
"The Gray Dots Down There are more
likely to eat it, defecate it, find it
a week later and eat it again."

As if to settle the argument,
God stirred, rolled over and
cleaved the OTHER in two
with a stroke of lightning.

God's Will was
satisfied. IF
the OTHER was
so interested in
duality, let him
hop around as two
people.

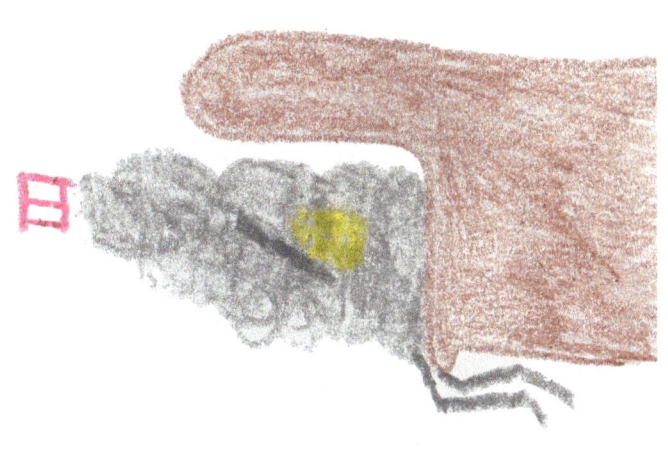

Meanwhile, the Gray King sat upon his throne, having trouble passing the lump of golden lion he'd eaten. The Gray King grit his teeth and kept telling himself "Enlightenment is worth it."

The OTHER's halves tried slapping themselves back together with limited success.

"What part of me are you?" asked one half of the OTHER Other.

"That's a dumb question," replied the Other OTHER. "Correctly posed: What part of me are you?"

Their interest in unification faded in favor of the argument.

There were points to be scored after all.

The Lion's essence was equally troubled. the Gray King King could stomach any thing but could process nothing.

His hope of passing on the Touch of God was dashed.

He wanted nothing now, except to accede to the Throne.

Whatever it was, thought God, making it out of Grey dirt only guarantees the smell.

Popping open a cloudy eye in mid-slumber, God saw the results of the half-OTHERS' argument... a mud man, grey earth kicked and patted into a massive shape.

But the half-OTHERS
were just being practical.

Dirt was the only material
plentiful enough for the job.

If they'd lived on a planet
of gold, it would look nicer,
but the job would be longer.

The half – OTHERS shaped the grey dirt by slapping their incomplete halves against it.

Sometimes, as one fell away from the moment of impact, it seemed to the other OTHER that it was a whole OTHER there, hanging in space, the mystic half momentarily completed by a dark grey half, rich moist soil soon to be dried by the sun.

Their age-long argument had come
to this crucial, shared question:
Was it possible to get God's attention
without drawing his wrath?

The Lion had
challenged Him
and was cast
out...

The Grey Kings had
threatened His High
office and were struck
down.

Certainly, God looked upon them on occasion, but the half-OTHERS felt they were no more noticed by God any more than they could look upon the land and notice a particular photon.

Could they catch God's eye and make Him smile? This, the half-OTHERS agreed, was a point worth exploring.

They wanted to make an impression. What better way is there than with an image?

The simplest way to draw God's eye would be his own image. Whose eye doesn't stop at one's own likeness?

But sightings of God were at best unreliable. The Lion was the best witness yet, but he was busy strangling the intestines of a tenth generation of Grey Kings.

Indeed, as the half-OTHERS sought their path to God's good graces, the line of Grey Kings since the Grey King King had been busy accessing the Divine by looking inward, and forcing a few ounces of undigested gravy from meat into any space they found in there.

Not one orifice on any of the nine Grey Kings since had proved adequate to processing the Divine Protein.

When the hole opportunities ran out, a Grey Queen was suggested, but there were no takers.

Soon, the job became un-palatable to even the most ambitious Grey, and the crown sat alone on the throne, itself crowned with the golden cypher, a hunk of the Divine so far unwilling to share itself with the world below.

The next time God stirred, he saw the giant mud man was complete, including two saucer eyes that seemed to look right through Him.

On its forehead were the half-OTHERS, with their vase of divinity distilled from the lion's point of impact.

He had the lightning ready before he'd formed the intent.

The mud man would become imbued with life and start hauling down clouds to use like a rocky cliff-face to rise and challenge Him.

But all the mud man did was stare with two black grey eyes, and a new eye-- a pool of the divine within an iris of the mystic and mundane.

The moment He blew apart the vase and the half-OTHERS, God knew he'd done the whole lion thing all over again.

Meanwhile, the Greys tried
putting the crown on top of
the Holy Remains and waited
for inspiration.
Things still had to be done, so
they created jobs to keep the
Grey World moving. If the
hunk of gluey meat over had
any directives, that would be
fine.

God stared past sleep, past pain, past understanding. The mud man never moved. It was just waiting for God to blink, thought God.

After a few more ages, God felt oddly soothed by the mud man's unending gaze. It was something He could always count on. Even though the mud man's goal was to destroy Him (probably), God began to look forward to that day.

It would make all the waiting worth while.

76

Interview: The JIT

in conversation with C. Anne Wells

This interview was conducted at the Quaker Square Inn, in Akron, Ohio on May 20, 2000. The JIT had contacted me directly the week before with a pointed request and something of a compliment. "As the only remotely sane writer on the JIT, I want to answer any question you have." He was an admirer of my August 1989 TIRE *essay "Man and the Absence" and a student of Greek Philosophy himself. Typical of the JIT, the interview started with him asking the first question.*

JIT: What made you say yes to this? I bet not one other person on the planet with my drawing on the wall would have done the same.

CAW: *I suppose it's because I'm an admirer of dialogue. You're not some remote source of knowledge. You're right here.*

JIT: In a motel. In a chair.

CAW: *The picture can't be the only knowledge you hold, that you can impart.*

JIT: But you don't think I can consciously impart it, right? That's part of your point. The knowledge intersects with me in a way different than the way it shows up in the rest of the world.

CAW: *That's the Platonic way of looking at it.*

JIT: What if that peek up reality's skirt has a time dimension? Maybe only I could have done it, but only at that specific time. That's [Celine] Taylor's idea. He was the only one who suggested that maybe there was no value in hassling me for twenty years and running.

CAW: *You're speaking of Celine Taylor's "A Moment Gone—Sunday is Past"* [TIRE, June 1988].

JIT: He proved that the JIT crowd can have an apostate.

CAW: *There is a rumor that you are the author of that article.*

JIT: Which is apparently the most damning form of disagreement among you people, to accuse them of being the JIT. Horrors!

CAW: *Yet he hasn't surfaced since, and noone in the JIT movement has ever met him.*

JIT: I can't account for the guy's social life. I offered him the interview and he backed away like the rest. He's a true believer.

CAW: *So, to be clear, you are not Celine Taylor.*

JIT: I'm no more him than I am you.

CAW: *I suppose it's no use to try to pin you down on this.*

JIT: The knowledge you seek doesn't come from me in any literal sense. The devil is in the details. The rest is in what's left.

CAW: *You've tried a few times to install youself as an official part of the JIT.*

JIT: By using JIT that way you're referring to the movement and not the man. JIT without John.

CAW: *Yes.*

JIT: I can't believe I'm making this comparison, but if Jesus actually showed up, would he be shut out of his own church? Would they plug up their ears, for fear that he might say something that wrecks their religious construct? Do they think he'll contradict his own holy word?

CAW: *I think many would say that they seek the truth behind the being. They might have a point in avoiding such an encounter. Whether real or not, claims of such visitations are usually accompanied by radically different messages than were previously presented.*

JIT: So it's the time thing again. Jesus of the year zero is good, but new Jesus, better tasting than the old Jesus, is week old bread. So why does the JIT actively shun the John?

At best, to you, I'm irrelevant.

CAW: *Where knowledge appears once, it might do so again.*

JIT: You're hedging your bets.

CAW: *The JIT has many members of various Christian denominations. I think your metaphor earlier might be better if you cast yourself as Mary rather than Jesus.*

JIT: You have to be yanking my chain.

CAW: *Let's get back on track. Have you tried Jitting beyond your* MEGA-CONTEMPLATIONS *volume?*

JIT: Just recently. I'm not gonna talk about that here. You'll get to see it.

CAW: *Why did you publish* MEGA-CONTEMPLATIONS?

JIT: Money. Also, it's extremely fun to insist that people who want to give me their crazy Jesus tract take it in trade. They never see it coming.

CAW: *How long has that been going on?*

JIT: Since about a minute after I published it. You're making a mental connection. What is it?

CAW: *Well, have you heard of Pillar Point Church?*

JIT: Glass and steel TV church in one of the Carolinas. Rev. Emanuel

Po, the Asian guy with space-alien plastic surgery.

CAW: *Yes.*

JIT: He's been running with it a bit. He'd like to steal the JIT business right away from you.

CAW: *Their* PILLAR TO POST *newsletter has clear influence of the JIT.*

JIT: Maybe one of my trades scored a direct hit. He's not going any farther than he has. That guy was easy to fix.

CAW: *You stopped him?*

JIT: I made sure he saw my two part column in the Texas Tech student newspaper from '90 "Who Has Rights? Fetuses Don't, Women Do" [*Texas Tech University Daily*, 9-10 April 1990]. No Carolina TV megachurch is gonna get that all over them. He has the opposite problem that the JIT do. I could have buddied up with that guy and made a bundle.

CAW: *Why didn't you?*

JIT: Because being someone's highly-paid monkeyboy sounds great until they measure you for the outfit they make you wear. You look at the tiny hat and the organ grinder and think a mop job at a Korean grocery would be better than this.

CAW: *So it wasn't that your book somehow made it into Rev. Po's*

hands.

JIT: I mailed it around. Fresh material is hard to come by for people doing the same book report every Sunday.

CAW: *You've long claimed that all you've wanted was a profitable role in the JIT. That seems contradictory.*

JIT: Po's people aren't the JIT. They're Po's. Look, if you've even a little famous, you want to keep your audience. The JIT will be into me long before anyone ever thinks it's cool.

CAW: *That's a dangerous notion for a living accessible source of the mysteries to have.*

JIT: Only for me. You're in no danger from it. I could paint myself into a corner like Alexander of Abuonoteichos and have to choose between being dead and believed or alive and just another asshole who says he's Pythagoras but won't jump into a fire to prove it. But since you people only seem to want some other moment of my life from me, some subtle, intangible thing I can't quantify, monetize, or miss, then what's the harm in having me on board? Am I to be a martyr?

CAW: *I want to shift to your role-playing now. You ran a superhero role-playing group continuously for about twelve years, first in Texas, then in Iowa.*

JIT: Was one of them a JIT?

CAW: *What makes you say that?*

JIT: Hell, maybe all of them were. I did plenty of weird crap to them. Who else would sit still for that?

CAW: *Biblical Miracle Magic.*

JIT: Ah, that.

CAW: *It was the notion that certain people could replicate in whole or in part miracles from the Bible. It worked like a magic spell, apparently.*

JIT: Yeah. The idea was that if all the world's other religions could be boiled down to Magic Missile, then why not Christianity? There's plenty of real world precedent. There are all manner of surviving attempts to create love charms and amulets based on tapping the power of Yahweh. Curses, even. Dear God, make my cheating husband's prick fall off. I just jumped up the power levels.

CAW: *No player ever got to wield it, though.*

JIT: So?

CAW: *So the power always stayed with the game's own god, the gamemaster, and his non-player proxies.*

JIT: You're accusing me of hypocrisy in an RPG? I might actually be offended. Look, I was just trying to make a point with Biblical Miracle Magic. Before I took the effort to sort out what Bible passage inspired me to make the drawing, I always believed that if the Christian worldview had any effect in this reality, it could be tapped. The Samarians are hotwiring a lion to find out what God wants.

CAW: *The God of the King.*

JIT: **2 Kings**, it turned out, is loaded with Biblical Miracle Magic. Elisha is a straight-up wizard. Dr. Strange was tight with Cytorrak; Elisha was tight with Yahweh. One has crimson bonds; the other has lions and bears. So I had grasped a truth about the text all those years ago, and carried it through my life. It instantiated in admittedly curious ways, but I stand by it. You want the knowledge behind the picture, the JIT, the Jitting, and all that? It's that a world with power is malleable. The question is, is this a world with power?

CAW: *Is it a world with power?*

JIT: Has Jitting changed anything? It made a few people some money. It jacked up my life. Worrying about its influence made me make more than a few unforced errors in my life. A group of otherwise unconnected strangers exert a subtle yet towering influence in everything from crazy made-up Jesus churches to a probate showdown that shook the tire industry. This world is humming with power. It's the magic of belief. Belief isn't the fuel for divine power.

It's an organizing force on the material world. It's not the means. It's the end. I didn't declare myself the JIT. I am the JIT because that's what people believe.

CAW: *Let's shift to Whitney Allen Turner.*

JIT: That guy wants to be the JIT in the worst way.

CAW: *He initially did try to claim the title, but it didn't take.*

JIT: I confess, that guy's existence makes me feel better about my lot in life. He wants a faceless cadre tailing him in the worst way. I told him there are a million easier ways to get famous.

CAW: *He's taken to calling you the Anti-JIT in recent tracts.*

JIT: I've tried like hell to be the Anti-JIT. He's not wrong about that. I suggested he call himself the WhAT, but that was a dirty trick of the Anti-JIT. Insert ten-foot pole here. If I told him to keep breathing, he'd be in the paper the next day.

CAW: *You've tried to help him? The things he says about you are strong stuff.*

JIT: To you. Someone runs around telling people you're not a prophet— what's hurtful about it? If I told a dog it was a terrible engineer, it would just keep wondering if I had food. It's irrelevant to my experience.

CAW: *I suppose he's helping you, in a way.*

JIT: If he peels one JIT off the pile, that's one less guy trying to steal my hair.

CAW: *And yet earlier you expressed some satisfaction in the JIT's brand of appreciation.*

JIT: You are what you love, not what loves you back. I'm surprised you haven't accused me of being the WhAT.

CAW: *At a certain point, you seem like the author of all of it. There's no logical place to stop doubting the reality of any of it.*

JIT: Hey, I am the JIT and the Anti-JIT. Metaphysically, how many other jobs are there?

CAW: *Are you trying to draw me in to this closed notion of the universe? You are the alpha and omega?*

JIT: You people can't decide what I am. I say I'm not your holy scribbler, I'm a 30 year old with a perfect notion of a nine year old rattling around inside him. I'm not your JIT. I'm not even its opposite. I'm emblematic of your own confusion about and hope for the world. Am I supposed to put on a sheet and take a bunch of wives? Do I put on a mass suicide? What am I supposed to do with you people? If I'm only to endure you, then I'm not your guy. I'm a martyr for your guy. Maybe Whitney's really your guy, and his holy struggle is the fact that nobody believes him. Tell me this. Do you believe Whitney? That he's the JIT and I'm the Anti-JIT?

CAW: *I do not believe he is the JIT. The JIT drew the drawing.*

JIT: So that's strictly an evidence-based decision for you.

CAW: *You've never denied drawing it.*

JIT: I've only denied its significance. I still draw like that. I couldn't deny it if I tried. So Whitney is not a source of that knowledge. He could know other things. I could screw the guy royally and accuse him of being the Anti-JIT. That would be an evidence-based assessment. He claims to have drawn the picture, despite never having lived in or near Lamar. He has an elaborate theory about how I ended up with the drawing, how I created the whole JIT movement all on my lonesome. He doesn't think you or anyone like you really exists. How does it feel to be a fictional being, someone I made up?

CAW: *But I'm not a fictional being.*

JIT: Whitney says you are. Go ahead and pinch yourself. It only proves you've real by your own perception. Batman thinks he exists, too. Otherwise, there'd be no point in trying to stop the Joker.

CAW: *Are you a nihilist? Is that the point of all this reductive talk?*

JIT: In a world where I'm the JIT, there actually is no goddamn point. If I'm the Anti-JIT, there's a good deal of fun to be had.

CAW: *And if you are both the JIT and the Anti-JIT?*

JIT: That's probably the world we're both in. You and me.

CAW: *Last question. Do you really think that this kind of knowledge falls upon people by accident? There are people who study the mysteries for decades who approach the knowledge it takes to decode the drawing, and nine year old you drew it on a whim. Can you not appreciate a design or at least a synchronicity in this?*

JIT: It's a manipulation of symbols. Words, pictures, all these marks we leave on things, they're symbols. They're the first special effects. No, second. Motion was the first. Symbols were the second. I matched symbols in a context that meant little to nothing to me. I'm the dog that will never design a bridge.

CAW: *To us, you're the dog who drew a bridge anyway.*

JIT: I have no idea how to respond to that. Do you want to pet me?

CAW: *Am I fictional?*

JIT: Yes. I made you up. Thanks for playing.

I'm Dock Bandero and I'm a palmist. I know, I must look like some dirty roughneck to you (especially in this picture!), but I make you this promise: I am a palmist.

I was never one to go for things like biofeedback, tripartite sentience training, or rubbing buckeyes for luck. But what I've discovered about the lines on your palm will shock even the experienced palmists. It may even anger some of you, and for that I do apologize. But I cannot be silent. The world is in sore need of knowledge, and I would be remiss if I kept this to myself and merely got rich off of something anyone could learn.

It came to me while I was driving through West Texas on my way to Boise City. I'd been on 87 north of Amarillo when I started thinking very clearly about fate. I'd been thinking about nothing at all and suddenly there it was in my mind: fate. It stuck with me all the way through Dumas, even up to Stanford. The experience was intense.

Getting out of the car in Boise City, my knees buckled and I fell to the ground. My mind was so filled with thoughts of fate that I couldn't even tell my legs to work! Coming back to the world after a bit, I thought about other travels through West Texas. There was that time driving from Borger to Stinnett where I thought only about success. In the aftermath of my meditation on fate, I was able to recognize the clarity and purpose of that memory.

There was the trip through Boys' Ranch, curving over to Dalhart. I had wondered with complete focus about how long I have left to live. The truths were coming thick and fast, almost too fast to comprehend. But their force and clarity pushed aside the irrelevant details and I was forced to a startling conclusion. There is a parallel between the West Texas highway map and the lines on every human's palm.

The basic lines are easy enough to see, once you look.

—87 from Amarillo to Stratford is the line of fate.

—136 from Borger to Gruver is the line of fortune.

—385 from Vega to Dalhart is the life line.

Once I correlated the known palmistry lines, there were lines on the map, roads on the ground that demanded investigation. The results will astound you!

My book is called **WEST TEXAS IN MY HAND** and it is the future of palmistry. You will be amazed to learn that there are TWO lines of the head, 352 from Channing to Junction 152 AND 136 from Fritch to Borger. Is it coincidence that the line of the heart begins in Hartley? You can believe it's chance, but to learn you must first believe!

You won't be able to grab a map and know these new truths. The only place to get them is in my book, **WEST TEXAS IN MY HAND**. You can find this book at any reputable New Age bookstore, or ask your local store to order you a copy. It will be worth the effort! For what comes to us without effort? If you would like a signed copy, send $25 to me at:

DOCK BANDERO

Amarillo, TX 79102

WHERE HAVE YOU BEEN?

Your current life may be influenced by decisions you made in a past life, when you were a very different person. We are not the same throughout our lives. They may well have been you in some form, but they were also unique individuals with unique choices and unique lives. Those lives had an impact on other people, who may be tangentially influencing your current life for reasons buried in the past. Feeling charmed? Everything going your way? A love from a past life may be unknowingly clearing the way in this life for you! Nothing goes right? Someone with a past grudge may be the cause.

Our staff of psychics, mediums, and genealogists can assemble a dossier and Life Path Chart for you based on details from your current life and our patented DNAfter test, which identifies the unique psychic strands that connect you to past and future lives. Current technology only permits us to identify past lives, but we do have a waiting list for people who want to be the first to know about their future lives when the time comes.

DNAfter testing can be done by you in the comfort and safety of your own home. We send you a kit with a DNAfter test stick. You go anywhere you please to find a stick you feel matches it in as few or as many ways as you perceive. You then grasp one stick in each hand and meditate on the earliest clear memory you have. The clearer and more real the memory, the more accurate the test sample will be. You then secure the sticks in the provided sample tubes and put them in the postage-paid envelope to send to us at Shrine Labs. The sticks will be compared, measured, astrally washed, and then burned for your privacy (as well as to collect valuable smoke pattern messages). After that, our team gets to work!

Any strands discovered by the DNAfter test are verified and thoroughly researched. Our mediums scour the planes looking for the spirits of suspected connections to rule out false positives while our channelers make contact with uninstantiated spirits who knew you before, to get the information they don't print on census forms or death certificates. If any uninstantiated spirits hold a grudge against you, we tag them to make them easy to spot on this plane of existence. You don't want someone with a grudge coming after you in a much younger body!

We also work to identify those who loved you at one time or another. Sometimes this love carries over into other lives. Can't find that special someone? Still relying on chance meetings to find your past life mate? That's a surefire path to dying alone and starting the cycle all over again. If the past life love isn't to your current taste, you can keep your distance and place your life at an oblique angle to theirs and reap the benefits of that strange feeling they have about you that makes them want to help you. We are very discreet!

If your grudge spirit is already instantiated in the world, we offer counseling to make them understand that their irrational feelings are simply the result of faulty chemistry in their minds and connect them with therapists who are eager to prescribe pills that will even out their mood and effectively sever their past life strand from their current consciousness. If your grudge spirit doesn't comply, we will provide you with full information about this person so you can be prepared. Information is key!

Don't let lifetimes of information and potential power go to waste! You're back for a reason! Let us help you find it! Quest Assistance, Old Man On The Mountain Advice, and Chosen One Goal Prioritization Packages available! Send $49.95 for DNAfter test kit and basic results package! Live your lives to the fullest! Don't wait for your next life to find out the answers! Write now!

Shrine Labs
████ ███ ███ ███ ███., Risen Sun, NM 87036

THE MARKS BENEATH:
New JIT Revelations!

What is it about this picture? A lot of people have tried to explain it to me, and I remain unconvinced. They patiently explain that since I am the conduit for the knowledge, that of course the truth of it would seem trivial to me. I didn't fall into a trance or enter some mantic state to draw the thing. I was nine.

The original is in marker, but in my adult jitting I have chosen crayons as my tools. Part of it is that crayons seem more appropriate to reacquire a child's mindset. But the truth is markers just aren't as awesome as they once were. I have no explanation as to why I feel that way. I can conclusively prove that erasers were way better then, but the marker assessment is strictly opinion.

The God of the King is going into the lion's body. The lion didn't merit capitalization then. There are other

The original. Try not to freak out.

details here that might be new to you, as this is a scan of the original. The copy that's been circulating for the last twenty years was of a photograph taken of the original in a frame. The magic of scanners now reveals more detail in the drawing.

Look under the blue table, the one with the lion on it. There are half-erased pencil marks. Don't blame erasers. I was a hasty artist as a child. This sort of remnant is common for me. I've been back through the whole *TIRE* archive and this detail never appears in any of the reproductions.

It looks to me like a wide-set pair of legs in shoes, meant to frame a view of someone in front of a table. I see a left arm and a head. To the left, there's an urn, or a chalice, or maybe something I was going to draw some fire on.

I also see the scale and detail problems that led me to trash most of my grade school drawings out of

Might be time to freak out a little.

pure disgust. An Art teacher who told me I was a bad artist didn't help things. The drawing was going to be too small, overall. Perhaps the message was to be different, too.

The original layout remnants invalidate the notion that the drawing was meant to be exactly as it is. That sinks articles by Morton ("The Vessel and the Water," *TIRE*, June 1982), Salmoni ("The Determined Line," *TIRE*, September 1984), and Witt ("As If No Artist," *TIRE*, February 1986).

I'm certain that I drew in the cockeyed penmanship lines after I'd finished drawing. That means that the immortal phrase "The God of the King is going into the lion's body" was a post facto explanation. The lines are skewed to fit the already delineated space. There are also unnecessary extra lines drawn in to fit more text.

That spells tough shit for Cruden ("In The Beginning Were The Words," *TIRE*, October 1992), Donnelly ("Eleven Words, Three Worlds," *TIRE*, March 1991), and Mireau ("The God of the King's UFO Connection," *TIRE*, November 1982). If Donnelly still wants to claim that "lion's" is "lion3," then I'm gonna let him have that.

I may have started the drawing by thinking about what I'd learned, but the result is clearly something I wish I'd learned instead. The word choice is uncomfortable to read as an adult. At nine, there's no odd sexual connotation. When I say it aloud to people now, there's an uncomfortable moment where they think that the picture might be scatological or obscene.

The assumption is that to be thrown out of Sunday School, I must have drawn something naughty. When they realize that it's simply weird and possibly a bit defiant to the original mandate, there's a moment of sympathy for that nine year old.

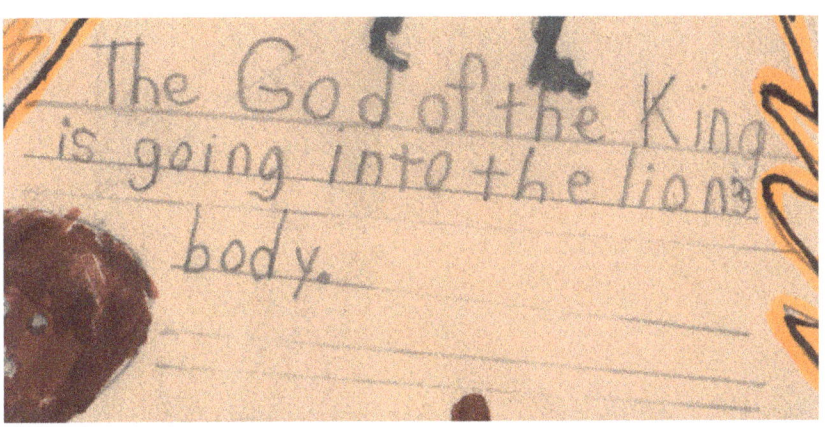

Was there more to say? Probably. We'll never know.

We've all garbled directions before. But I definitely did not err. I drew what I wanted.

At right is more revealed detail. The lion's claws remained in pencil, because I suspect that I found drawing them in with marker to be too difficult. If I had, they'd have been thick as fingers, which wouldn't look right on a lion. Plus it would have made Feddersen ("Which is the Lion, and Which the King?", *TIRE*, January 1994) look slightly less stupid, and who would want to do that?

There are another pair of legs, or perhaps it's a too-skinny table. It's possible that the original picture was going to be an eyewitness view of things from behind two people participating in the ceremony. A lot of my early drawings were attempts to get several views of the same object into one picture. In Kindergarten I remember trying to fingerpaint the Hall of Justice from the *Superfriends* cartoon from the front and from the point of view of a flag flying on top.

Above the lion's paw is another shape. Most likely it was an attempt to show the lion's back legs. I often questioned these style choices and erred on the side of simplicity when I could. For instance, the figure in black at left of the lion seems to have only one leg. Note to Erlich ("Black Man, Blue Man," *TIRE*, August 1993)—he does. Further note to McQueary ("The Man with Three Legs by the Fire," *TIRE*, January 1996)—those are not extra legs. They are arms drawn by a nine year old. Even for this crowd, you're

Think about the picture that could have been.

reaching.

To the left of the lion, there are clear indications that his table was supposed to be wider, but that I had thought better of it. The diagonal lines going up and into the man in black's arm may be some notion of binding for the lion. A lion's not going to sit still for this business, after all.

At bottom are the legs, suggesting where the lion originally lay in the drawing. The lack of boots suggests this to me. I drew animal paws as if they were the curved part at the end of a leg. Originally, the lion did not face the viewer. The final position of the lion was unusual for me, as I was always more comfortable drawing faces in profile.

Seeing this part blown up, I'm going to admit that Hoffman ("The JIT's Connection to Easter Island," *TIRE*, December 1984) might be on to something with the man in black's head. His conclusion that I am in fact a reincarnated Polynesian who watched guys from Mars carve giant heads suddenly doesn't sound so weird or stupid. I have met Hoffman, though, and he's pretty weird and stupid. So he's got a long row to hoe, there. I'm rooting for you, Hoffman!

There are more stray pencil strokes in the rest of the picture: an attempt to add a strut to the torch on the right, some fire action lines over the torch on the left, some more zaps. But there's one more detail that I want to show you, and a serious revelation attached to it. Take a breath, Jitters, before you turn the page. You will not believe your eyes.

Does your theory still work?

89

This is under the King's table, almost too light to see. It says "John T," except that's not my handwriting. I drew the picture, but someone else signed my name to it. Was it the Sunday School teacher? It wasn't my parents. Their handwriting was much better than this.

I present this to you as the final mystery of the JIT. I wanted to get out in front of the pencil lines revelation and essentially piss in the JIT research well again. They're incredibly meaningful and add richness and depth to JIT scholarship. Or they are meaningless and should be ignored. Or they are latter day additions by the artist in an attempt to paralyze JIT scholarship. Or they are additions by other hands, seeking to pollute the JIT. Or they are the work of the Anti-JIT. Or they are the work of another child, and the artist drew over these inferior lines. Or Hoffman's right and it's all still about Easter Island. Or the JIT is the wrong term to use, and JohnT should be used instead. Or the JohnT is the pencil artist and the JIT is the marker artist. Maybe the JIT and the JohnT are the same person. Maybe the JIT and the JohnT are different people.

I could do this all day long.

—*John Ira Thomas*
The JIT, The Anti-JIT, The JohnT,
The Man in the Moon, The Witness
At Rapa Nui, The Pisser in the Well

ιDATIVE BOOKS *"Books of use"*

If you think you have the skills to survive, think again! Only the prepared have a chance, and the only place to learn what you need to know is here! Dative Books are exhaustively researched and 100% accurate. We only publish books that are useful. If we know it, someone who means to exploit you may know it too. Be prepared! Stay ahead! All volumes available whever books of truth are sold.

CRAFTING IRREGULAR WASHERS by Haggard Veyard—a guide to poorly made washers the specific size and weight of quarters. For amusement purposes only.

EXPLOITING THE MAGSTRIPE by Inez Varra—The magnetic stripe is the wax tablet on which you can write your own ticket. Learn to rewrite tracks and make portable regaussing tools. For amusement purposes only.

REMIXING HIGHS by Dr. Henry Tsuras—Explains legal highs and pre-schedule substances. Know what works and how to make stategic chemical adjustments to old favorites. For amusement purposes only.

HACKING HEAVEN by Oriana Chen—Explore usable paths to post-existence glory with a guide to religions with late belief buy-ins and heavy conversion favorability. For amusement purposes only.

THE DEVIL'S MESSAGES by MC Steve Logleich—Get to the real messages in rock music! Learn how to play the third side of an LP and decode the data missing from the center of a CD. For amusement purposes only.

24 HOUR PRIMROSE by Erica Korl—Learn how to live in a big box store undetected! Problems such as strategic food acquisition and covering your tracks are addressed. For amusement purposes only

UNDER THE GRID LIVING by Hobo Mike—Learn the ways and wonders of the world below the streets! Subjects include navigating sewers, barter methods, learning to tell a grinch grunch from a spinach winach. For amusement purposes only.

Y2K FACTION BUILDING by Garman Whittleford—It won't take much to be a powerful faction when the knot at the center of civilization is untied. Be small, nimble, powerful. SURVIVE! For amusement purposes only.

CULT DEPROGRAMMING by Bettina Carlsen—Why spend time and energy deprogramming one cult member when you can join and cause a schism! They get their kid back, and you get the rest of them! Not everyone has a home to go back to. For amusement purposes only.

FINDING YOUR SEX WORK NICHE by Adam Adams—At last, a cleareyed checklist to help you find your unique appeal. Why give it away? It might not even be sexual to you. For amusement purposes only.

YOGA FOR COMBAT by Srinivas Orlinsky—The media would have you believe that yoga is about peace and serenity, but the philosophy was bolted onto a strength and combat system rivaling the training of ninja! Learn the truth! For amusement purposes only.

DON'T WAIT! SOMEONE ALREADY KNOWS ALL OF THIS!

91

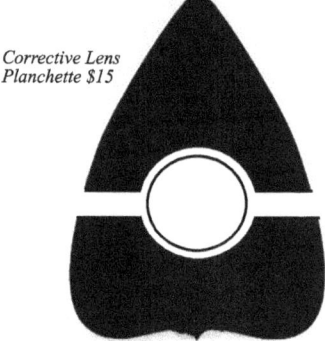

YOUR STEVENSON POLAR SIGN INDEX FOR JULY 2000

What should you and your bad self expect in July?

ARIESLIBRA (*The Scaly Ram*)—Travel should be restricted to foot-powered vehicles only. Luck will find you in a pedalcar this month! *It's a good time for you to mug someone. Look for some fool who's out of place and take what's theirs!*

TAURUSCORPIO (*The Stinging Bull*)— Curb your impulsiveness this month. It's a good time to look at your household budget. *Ponder the long con this month. It's more effort, but the payoff is bigger. Try flipping houses.*

GEMINITTARIUS (*The Double-Shafted Arrow*)—Your partner is your focus this month. The stars suggest there may be trouble in a relationship. *Waiting to break it off? July is the time. If you don't have a current relationship, start one now and end it in July.*

CANCERCORN (*The Crabby Goat*)—Your health will be good, as long as you do not overeat or drink to excess. Moderation! *This is a good time to test your limits. See how drunk you can get someone.*

LEOQUARIUS (*The Wet Lion*)—July will be a creative month for Leoquarians! Start a new project, but stick to it. *Tell a creative person that if they were any good, they'd be rich. They have to hear this from someone. It might as well be a Leoquarius!*

VIRGOPIS (*The Untouched Fish*)—Don't make any big purchases in July. Best to wait out the mess in Mercury's House. *Know what's cheap in July? Everything. Get out there and acquire!*

Smoke signs (Areslibra, Geminittarius, Leoquarius) should beware of law enforcement in general in July. Mud signs (Tauriscorpio, Cancercorn, Virgopis) should embrace the variable interest rate. Balloon payments are nothing to fear. Learn more about the SPSI and valuable information about the untapped value in your home! Send for FREE booklet!

SPSI, ▬▬▬ Okamucha, FL 34448

ARE YOU READY?

The Iowa Space Command is making its first launch to Inner Space! From our launchpad in Johnson County, we are ready to send a human craft inside the world we know! **Will it be you?** We are holding intranaut tryouts in six counties across Iowa in the month of August! Select candidates will be subjected to a grueling series of tests to prove their worthiness as a planar vessel. If you think you have what it takes, come see us at:

The Duolith in
Verge, IA
August 1

The Fancy Faire in
Stolen Oak, IA
August 7

The Silver Where in
Cartilage, IA
August 11

The Casey's in
Porcine Reach, IA
August 14

The Hotel Masada in
East Des Moines, IA
August 21

The KOA Campground
east of South Liberty, IA
August 28

YOU DO NOT NEED AN APPOINTMENT, but you must have our assessment form already filled out when you arrive. For form and further information, send $5 to:

IOWA SPACE COMMAND
▬▬▬
Manly Junction, IA 50456

WHO LOSES BETTING ON THE DOGS?

You do! Did you know that greyhounds participate in a pack-mind intelligence bent on bankrupting the best among the human race? Or that they do this as part of a sinister three-point plan to prevent you from reaching your full potential? Admit it. You've lost a few bucks at the dog track. There's no shame in admitting it. But you should be ashamed of yourself if you pass up this important wisdom! We must stop the greyhounds' nefarious plot to slow and ultimately halt the evolution of Man. Why do they do this?

TO CATCH UP.

They know that if Mankind stalls, the breed will have the time they need to overtake us! They're already faster and leaner than we'll ever be. You could exercise like a man possessed for the rest of your life, and you'd never be as skinny and fast as a greyhound. All they need is a litter of pups with prehensile paws and the game will be OVER! We can't destroy the greyhounds. They're too numerous. We could never be sure we got them all. The only thing we can do is

TAP INTO THE GREYHOUND PACK-MIND!

With meditation and dedication, it can be done. With our seven steps on the ladder to Canine Intelligence, you can help stop this insidious plot! What can the dogs know that we don't, you may ask. Our brains are bigger. They have no culture, no literature, no monuments to their greatness. But that's what makes them dangerous.

OUR BRAINS ARE TOO BIG!

We overshot the ideal brain size by about one million years. There's too much going on up there, too many distractions. What did you do today to advance Mankind? How about yesterday? We can't shrink our brains, or turn back the evolutionary clock. Critical mental functions are too evenly distributed in our brains. There's no going back now.

WE CAN'T KNOW OUR EARLIER EVOLUTIONARY SELVES.

That ship has sailed. But we can access an earlier evolutionary mind. Enter the greyhound pack-mind and unlock the doors before they do! We already have the hands, the complex digits.

WE CAN WIN THIS RACE!

Once atop the seven step ladder of Canine Intelligence, we can pivot and take the journey that should have happened before Jesus, before the siege at Troy, before government, before society!

IT ALL BEGINS WITH THEIR CURRENT PLAN!

The thing you never suspected, that no-one could have suspected, is the shocking truth at the center of the greyhounds' plan.

THEY DECIDE WHO WINS EVERY RACE!

They know about the scouting reports. They know their race histories better than any tip sheet. You think they care about a fake slot-car rabbit? That's what they

WHAT IS THE DOGS' MASTER PLAN?

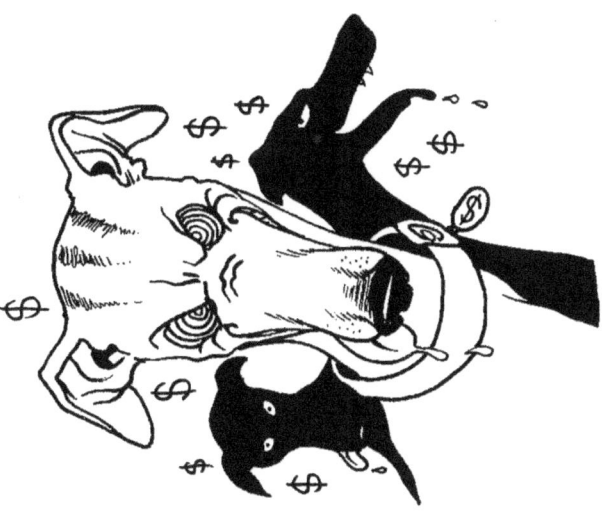

want you to believe!

WHAT'S THE POINT OF THEIR PLAN?

To demoralize you! They want you to think you can't master a simple dog race! They want you to lose money in the process, to ruin your life! They want you to stop believing in the potential of Mankind! Most of all, they want YOU to deny yourself your rightful place as a future leader of Mankind.

IT'S NOT TOO LATE FOR YOU! JOIN THE GREYHOUND PACK-MIND!

Start winning at the track! Use that money to better yourself and thus better Mankind! Get Rich! What better way is there to help the world than by erasing frivolous concerns like debt and want? And where's the best place to start erasing these concerns? With you!

THE WISDOM IS HERE!

Send no money now. We will send you information on the first step of Canine Intelligence FREE OF CHARGE. If you can't wait for the mailman, you can get the first and second steps right now by calling 1-900-DOG-HEAD (connection charges apply).

FIGHT THE PACK-MIND

~~Pasadena~~, Santa Anita, CA 91007

1-900-DOG-HEAD

TURN YOUR LIFE AROUND!
SAVE HUMANITY!
START WINNING AT THE TRACK!

𝐼𝑡 𝐻𝑎𝑝𝑝𝑒𝑛𝑒𝑑 𝑇𝑜 𝑀𝑒
by Our Readers

When sifting through the TIRE *slush pile, I found a lot of the usual mystic encounter bunk. For the final installment of this feature, I selected only follow-up accounts to previous entries. There are varying levels of regret in all of them. Some are suffering because of the attendant attention; some feel they've misjudged their experience; and some want to have a do-over to claim something even more insane. Since this issue is about my own second look at the JIT experience, I thought it only appropriate to let some other folks have their second bite of the apple.*

First up is Greta Gathers of Manly, Iowa. She writes: I wish to retract all claims of having seen Lonfoot [*TIRE*, May 1997]. The attacks are more frequent now, and I don't see him every time. I think that he may be part of my imagination after all. The only consistent experience I have now is the vision

of the Flowing Valley (rendering enclosed).

Perhaps Lonfoot is like me, someone who visits the Flowing Valley during attacks. Perhaps he is another human, having an experience beyond his ability to process, and I look to him like a Lonfoot. I think instead of a cryptid, I am looking at my soulmate. Perhaps his experience is of being chased by Lonfoot, as he has always run from me when I seek him out. Perhaps I am the author of his terror, and this I cannot bear to be.

I wish to blot out the Flowing Valley, and enter it no more. The ECT I have refused for so long seems the best way to accomplish this. I send you this in the hope that your readers do not inquire about the Flowing Valley again, so that they might not accidentally open the door in my mind again. If the Lonfoot I have seen reads this, know that I do this for you.

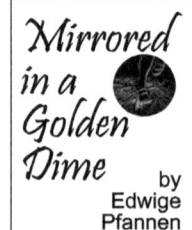

Ham Gausler of Lackawanna, Pensylvania writes: The Electric Ghost [*TIRE*, December 1976] haunts us no more. I spoke with an engineer among the English and we have worked together to trap this thing.

Repeated attempts by the English engineer had previously met with failure. He had used many electric tools and the Electric Ghost was unfazed by them. The task required metalwork from our blacksmith, as we could not use the tools of the English to rid ourselves of this entity. The process was difficult because the ductile metals involved melt at too low a temperature for the blacksmith's tools.

But with a different approach to the cooling process (air, not water), we were able to construct a trap that could be raised at a moment's notice. Once one of our neighbors sounded three rings on a bell, we could be there in minutes. It did not take long. The Electric Ghost had grown bold with the failures of the ways of the English to trap it.

Within a day after the trap's construction, Lemuel Barnaby sounded three bells before first light. Our trap was sprung and we hold the Electric Ghost even now. We are unable to move the trap without being burned, and when we use poles and planks to shift the trap, the Electric Ghost seems able to wriggle a bit of itself loose. So we shifted the road to the Barnaby house six feet over.

Suggestions are welcome as to the Electric Ghost's destruction or

98

WHO IS CONTROLLING YOUR LIFE?

WHO IS CONTROLLING YOUR LIFE? Are you a useful piece to Him? How long will you remain on the board? Who is He playing against? If you are a pawn, this knowledge tells you a wealth of information! A pawn that makes it to the other side of the board becomes any piece He chooses!

Will He choose a weak piece? No! Power awaits you at the far end of the board! Guided by His hand, you will take other pieces easily! You will move in new ways through life. FIND YOUR PLAYER! KNOW HIM! Send $10 for rules, movement chart. If He so moves you, you must write today!

The Ten Virtues of Solaricon Will Change You!

LEARN THE TRUTHS!

REALMING

OLDTONGUE

FEEL THE WARMTH!

GREENING

NEVERSING

LIFESHIFT

PASTDUMP

INNERFIRE

VESTALING

ACTIVEHAND

SUNKENEYE

$1 for first ray of Solaricon!

Ester, MD 21776

what secrets does the Internet hold?_

As more people confine their daily existence to the Internet, it will take on more of our characteristics. What will it be like when we've put enough of ourselves into it? Will it have its own thoughts, as if one giant mind, or will it become a country of its own, full of new people with no tangible form outside the computer? What will they want? We should not fear y2k! It may be our salvation! Read the account of one man who fell in love with one of these virtual people and judge for yourself! Buy SHE WAS NEVER REAL, by Anonymous2431. It's ten dollars for knowledge that may spare your heart, or your life!

Digital Ether Books

Porchlane, WA 98361

removal. The English engineer has included one of his photographs. While I do not approve of such things, the English insists it may be of help to you, and I am not so proud as to deny help to those who may need it.

Julie Eerdorn of Slapout, Oklahoma sent this followup on her psychic experiments. My beloved psychic hound, Bacon, has been dognapped! It was shortly after you published my testimony [*TIRE*, March 1987] about how Bacon knew his name before I ever said it to him. Just as God knew Job in the womb, Bacon knew his own name by looking into my mind.

My church told me that Bacon had supernatural powers, and was not of God. But God made Bacon, too! He's too good a dog to be doing anything ungodly. Bacon was on the

100

trail of a missing girl from the papers here [*Apparently this is Missy Irvil. See postscript.—JIT*], and I could tell there was something he didn't want to share with me.

He'd divined something important, caught an unguarded thought from someone. Bacon knew that knowledge could put me in danger. I tried everything to get it out of him: belly rubs, even his favorite treat (guess what that is!). The person who took that girl took Bacon too.

And I think that person must be me. Bacon's an indoor dog, and I'm the only person he ever sees. I must have done something to Bacon and that girl, but I don't know what. I need psychic help! Someone needs to read my mind to find out where Bacon and that girl are! I can't read my own mind.

PLEASE HELP!

Postscript: I looked into this one. Julie was exactly one house off on her search for Bacon. Fortunately, Julie also called the cops, as well as write to her favorite paranormal journal for help. They found Bacon at the home of Ronell Jenks. Bacon had used his psychic powers to locate the smell of, yes, bacon frying there. Ronell was making his new underage girlfriend Missy Irvil fry it for him.

When the cops found Bacon, they found Missy Irvil feeding Bacon bacon. After solving the crime of the century by the purest of coincidences, Julie decided that perhaps she'd gone a bit overboard on the whole psychic dog thing.

I'm kidding. There's an ad in back of this very issue where you can hire

Bacon to read the minds of or find any missing person located within a fifty yard radius of Julie's house. She weighs 600 lbs and has almost completely bonded permanently with her couch, so house calls are out, unless it's her house.

Hector Resvold of St. Marcel, Missouri writes: The Liquor Genie [*TIRE*, October 1998] is back! She just granted a wish to one of my customers by giving him that day's Pick Three numbers. He described the genie just like that last fellow. She looked at first like a person does when you look at them through a clear bottle. She shifted like you do in a funhouse mirror.

I've run the Liquor Spot and Maker Holler, home of fine spirits and craft supplies (new primitives classes starting soon!), for ten years. I've seen spirits steer people in all kinds of wrong directions, but I swear this genie means well. She always seems to catch people alone in an aisle. She don't show on the video, and even when someone cries out I can't never get there quick enough to see it. All I know is, some genie appears to be handing out good lottery numbers at the Liquor Spot and Maker Holler, corner of Third and Supply, in St. Marcel, MO.

Angela deSanigh of Advent, Nevada gets to be the last seeker ever in this column. I am writing again to cancel my late husband's lifetime subscription to *TIRE*. Your attempt to frame a simple subscription problem as a ghostly instance of *It Happened To Me* [*TIRE*, April 1994] is beyond appalling. A ghost does not exist simply because a subscriber is dead and does not cancel the subscription himself! Your magazine is the worst kind of dribble, worms mashed up in the beak of a looney bird, deposited neatly into the eager mouths of your willing subscribers.

Your magazine is a monthly reminder of my loss and the attendant difficulties. It's bad enough my husband mailed away his pension a few dollars at a time for opaque answers from turbaned housewives and photocopied manuals on jitting! Since you refuse to cancel his subscription, I am submitting a change of addess for him to your address. Now the ghost of my husband lives with you. Spooooky!

The hole that opens for you is rarely the right one. Learn to find the right hole. A door is either open or closed. A hole simply is. You are the traveler. The hole does not move. There are three exceptions. Send $10 to HOLIEST OF HOLES, ███████, Saker, SC 29010.

IMAGINATION IS THE KEY TO A HAPPY AFTERLIFE!

We talk of Heaven, but what we fear is Hell. All we really know of Hell is that it is a place of suffering beyond imagination. Those of us with good imaginations create intricate, terrifying visions of it. We work constantly to avoid it, and yet we know that a gap in our acts or our knowledge can send us there. What if the Bible were a clever blueprint to send billions to Hell with key omissions? Is it a coincidence that it does not mention abortion? All we know is that the horrors of Hell exist in direct proportion to our ability to grasp and picture it. Our imaginations must be brought under control! The Walk of Orpheus is the solution! With practice, exercise, and calculated drudgery, your imagination can be dulled and even silenced with the aid of our own Lethe Solution. Started after age seventy (or after a terminal diagnosis), the exercises and doses of the solution provide a gradual path to complete incomprehension of afterlife fears. The Devil will find nothing useful in your mind. If you don't get to Heaven, you can at least tolerate Hell. Send $5 for more information. If you fear the dark, invite the darkness inside your mind!

THE WALK OF ORPHEUS

~~P~~ ~~43 44~~

Marfall, FL 32321

103

How Could I But Survive?

TIRE pays $10 cash for every story published in this column. The story must be about an actual experience proving spiritual survival of the body. No fictional accounts are allowed. Letters for this column must be 300 words or less, typed, and include a self-addressed stamped envelope. They may be mailed to *TIRE* Spirit Editor ███████████████████████. [*Sorry, folks. Store's closed, but I found a few that I thought worth a Hamilton.—JIT*]

I AM A DOOR
By Ruden Fort Myers

IT WAS the man who said he wasn't a Rosicrucian. They always are when they say they're not. It wasn't the fact that he was a Rosicrucian that made me a door for spirits. It was merely the fact of him.

He had a spirit trapped in him, a boy who had died in a fire, who had struggled under burning timbers until his death. He was now trapped under the Rosicrucian, half buried in the man's corporeal form as he walked around, unaware. They seemed as though conjoined twins, the mortal man appearing shot through the bowels with the shimmering form of the struggling boy, his legs dangling upward as if his own gravity were pulling him to the sky.

In reaching for the boy's hand, I made a gesture to the mortal man as though I wished to touch him inappropriately. He resisted, but the boy did not. The boy's touch was electric. In an instant he slid free from the Rosicrucian and through me to I know not where.

I was so stunned by this that my reach extended past the boy and onto the Rosicrucian. He misunderstood, thinking me a groper, or as the Rosicrucians among the police call it, a serial groper.

They do not understand. Rosicrucians never do. I am a door. The spirit boy's freedom proves it. I repeat that electric moment often, in public (as before), reaching out to repeat that moment. People misunderstand. So many Rosicrucians!

A SPIDER WON'T MOVE
By Aurelia Porter

A GHOST has frozen a spider on my hand. Even as I type this letter, the spider will not move. The spider lives, but is motionless. I know it lives, because when I clear my mind and the room is quiet, I feel its living presence on me. When I clear my mind and try to sense the spirit, I cannot. This is how I know it is a spirit.

In the spider, throughout it, I feel its tiny life force. It is similar to the tickle from a hair, but I have learned the difference between that feeling and the jolt of life from the tiniest creatures. It is sudden, clean, and powerful, like the prick of a shiny pin in the center of one of my pores. The spider is alive.

The spirit resents this small, vital life force. A man who once lived, walked the earth, experienced the world, is now dead and so jealous of every living thing, that he has chosen this arachnid as the focus of his ire. He will not let it move. But the spirit still rages, for he knows that the spider still lives.

What if I were to smash the spider? What would the spirit do then? Would the spirit of the spider then seek its own revenge against something smaller than itself? Would it paralyze a single living neuron in my brain, taking away some small component of my thoughts and locking my brain down? Would that send my thoughts spiralling off to pointlessness? Has this already happened? I have killed spiders before.

Are all the spiders I killed each freezing one of my neurons? What would I be thinking if this wasn't true? I can't know. Would I know more? What if one freezes the neuron that makes me remember to eat, or go to the bathroom? When have I last eaten? I can't picture breakfast. Maybe the dead spiders took the idea of breakfast from me. I'm not sure what breakfast is, anymore.

A spider won't move, and I have forgotten breakfast again.

TIE THE KNOBS!
By Candy Berhnich

THIS IS important knowledge. Everyone who encounters spirits should know this. Find a rag. Put it in your pocket. It will save you from malevolent spirits! Put a rag in every pocket!

I am known around my town as a seeker of ghosts. Many are purely ambient instantiations of pure emotion emanating from the moment of death both forwards and backwards in time. They are easily more interesting than butterflies, but much easier to collect. Just cross the path of a ghost and you will carry an experience of their raw emotion with you forever. It's so much less cruel than sticking pins in poor butterflies!

I think that the more active ghosts may have been collectors, like myself. When a living person collects enough of these emotional memories experienced through spirits, they assemble something of a ghost in their living selves. They create a framework through which they can express themselves after their own passing. Perhaps I shall be a ghost. I will do my best to be nice to the living.

Encounters with the more organized ghosts can be terrifying. Some have specific goals in the world they no longer properly inhabit. Some just want to torment the living, as if the world were some fraternity that passes on hazing and terrible behavior to keep the older members from feeling like fools for agreeing to it in the first place.

When you encounter one of these damaged spirits, you must run! Do not let them imprint their nastiness on you. No collection should include such awful feelings. Beat your feet and put them in your rearview mirror.

Eluding ghosts is not easy. They pass with ease through material things. This is where the rags come in. To keep a ghost out of a room, tie a rag in a knot around the doorknob. They cannot use the door or even pass through the wall. The knotted knob evokes some crooked logic of the Other World. If the door is secure, the room is secure. It's as if their mortal imprinting kicks back in . . ."Well, if the door's locked, then I can't get in."

Use this knowledge! Create a ghost trap in your home! A closet is perfect. Get the ghost in there and tie a rag around the knob. He'll be trapped! Not so tough now, are you, ghost?

FORGOTTEN KEYS
By Steven Yorke

I COULDN'T for the life of me find my keys. My wife Irina always used to say "Durak! Put your keys where you find them later!" Ever since I brought her back from the Baltic Sea resort where we'd been introduced, my wife was always after me to keep track of my keys.

Ever since she passed away, she's still after me to keep track of my keys. "Can't find them again? Where did you put them?" I hear her all the time.

I've tried getting a dish to put them in. I tried using one of those valet stands. I've even tried hooks, with little success. My Irina still says "Put them somewhere you'll remember!"

Now I put them on the counter.

MAN IN FIRE ELECTED

Bushwa, AR (UPI) — Reports are circulating in an Ozark Mountain hamlet of a dancing man in a campfire there. The dancing man has been credited with preventing a number of wild cat attacks and predicting the outcome of a local pregnancy. Locals are restricting access to the fire, which they now feed day and night to keep the dancing man's protection upon the city.

Mayor Starla Brogham has declared the dancing man to be an honorary citizen of the city, and has even offered a local referendum to appoint this being a seat on the local city council. "The Dancing Man in the Fire stands for limited government," says Mayor Brogham. "He sees that its role is only to protect its citizens and provide knowledge of Other Planes whenever it's available."

The mayor believes that the federal government is keeping knowledge of extended realities to itself. The referendum is expected to pass, as most of the town is involved in the continuation of the fire. State officials had no comment.

YOU'RE NOT BUYING ANY OF THIS, ARE YOU?

Don't send anyone in this magazine any money before verifying their claims! If they won't offer proof, we will! We've tested thousands upon thousands of claims in ads in magazines just like this one! Learn to spot the fakes, the frauds, and the scams with our handy guides:

Finding the Right Astrologer

Questions to Ask Before Summoning

Is Everything I Know Wrong?

Consumer Guide to Divination Electronics

DON'T GET SCAMMED! We're here to help you find knowledge of other planes, summon spirits safely, or find the right device to weed out the weakness in you. All 5 guides $50 or $12 each. FREE SHIPPING TO THE CONTINENTAL U.S.

The Best Business Bureau

████ ████

Des Plaines, IL 60016

Jesus is born to us . . . it's time to raise Him right! The Baby Jesus awaits training! We are 2000 years in his future. There's so much we can teach Him! What would Jesus be like if He knew about movies and abortion? We can alter His timeline! He'll still die for our sins, but His teachings will be so much more relevant to modern life! We just need faith, dollars, and rare earth metals to make it happen!

LET'S RAISE JESUS
████, Gatling, VT 05055

What is the End?
Is it only the end for you?

That's no fun! Fifty percent of evangelicals believe the world will end in their lifetime. You think they're afraid of something other than God's wrath? They fear leaving the party early. The dead rising from the seas and emerging from graves is the cheap seats for people not born at the right time. How can you be sure that you'll be alive when the battle at Armageddon begins? By participating!

The last steps before seals start breaking involve building a temple where the mosque at the Temple Mount now stands! Some thinkers believe this mosque must be destroyed to make way for a new Jewish temple, but the Holy Word says nothing of the sort! It also doesn't say how big the temple has to be (Rev. 11:1-2), only that it can be measured.

We're experimenting with HO-scale (1:87 scale) temples placed atop the Rock, and are ready to try sizes from pillow-fort up to shed! As it says in Revelation, "do not measure the court outside the temple; leave that out." All that it requires is that it be a Jewish temple. It doesn't even have to stand for long. Once the right size church is erected in the right spot, the final act of mankind will begin! You'll be right there for all of it! Send a love offering of $50 and receive your very own HO-scale copy of the Third Temple!

Pastor Herriot Wilbaster
Church of the Acceleration
████, Occam, FL 32347

107

TOMES & PAMPHLETS

You could spend the rest of your natural life and a healthy chunk of whatever else you believe in looking through the TIRE *book reviewer's pile of unopened mail. I reviewed everything that hit the floor when I moved the guy's chair.—JIT*

DOGURY: Methods and Means of Sirian Divination by R. Teele, D. Ps., M. P. T. (Starways International, Portland, OR, 224 pages, $14.95)

Reading the flap, it seems that D. Ps. Is "Doctor of Psychic" and M. P. T. is "Master of Planar Travel." Reading the rest of the book doesn't net much more knowledge than that. Using one star (Sirius, the Dog Star, natch) for a complete system of Astrology seems like trying to suck an elephant through a straw to me. Also, would it kill R. Teele to include one picture of a dog? With a title like *DOGURY*, I had high hopes it was about predicting the future by watching dogs. If anybody runs out and writes that after reading this, I want a taste.

SOURCELICS: Mastering the Mind by David Rockley (Sourcelics Institute, Plainview, TX, 176 pages, $12.95)

I spent a lot of time trying to parse the title, to be honest. *SOUR CELICS*? *SOURCE LICS*? Best guess is it's an unholy etymological mashup of "source" and "sorcel," the verb form of "sorcery." And "-ics,"at least to David Rockley, means "Science!" Much of the book is spent talking up how minds are essentially tetherballs anchored to a pole of unshakable beliefs. The mind can stretch and pull, but it can't unmoor itself from the pole and, presumably, the abuse of grade school children at recess. Rockley does not suggest cutting the cord or uprooting the pole. Turns out he's rather fond of tetherball. Learning to wrap around the pole efficiently is his ultimate goal.

There are more books with a MadLib title of *THE UFO*-blank *CONNECTION* than can fit in the trunk of a decent-sized car. They are always an interesting shade of crazy, and are among the more single-minded texts you're likely to find. *THE UFO/UFO CONNECTION* connects ass to mouth and closes the system perfectly. The unnamed author (unless that triangular squiggle I see here and there is it) sees UFOs as a grand hoax perpetrated by any number of natual and supernatural cutouts. They're all here: Bigfoot to the Jersey Devil, Knights Templar to Knights of Malta, multi-planar beings to MK-ULTRA. Behind this vast conspiracy? It's UFOs. Right around the chupacabra/Bay of Pigs chapter, it feels like the thread was lost. Either the author forgot his original goal and there was only so much toilet paper left in the roll he was writing on, or he finally got his electro-convulsive therapy session, or he's just nuts. Right where Castro and the chupacabra who had once been Batista's lover (and co-owner of an unnamed Cuban casino pre-revolution) agree to build anti-landing pads to prevent planar travel anywhere in Cuba, that's where the book looks around and decides to wade back upstream.

THE EGYPTIAN BOOK OF THE LIVING, by Pharoah Gary (Myowndamn Books, Cairo, Egypt [*postmark is Moline, IL—JIT*], 154 pages, $1,000,000.00)

Like a lot of Pyramid Power books, this one has a carefully-wrought diagram of the Great Pyramid of Giza to serve as a combination scorecard and pivot point for its argments. This drawing never changes, as it is used to lend scientific credence to whatever anvil the author wants to bang on for 100-150 pages.

Pharoah Gary is not your average Pyramid Power guy. He adds a good many rooms to the Great Pyramid. They were once there, he explains, but the Great Pyramid is a work in progress, as a movable puzzle box. Subtle changes by man and nature have tripped internal changes. Rooms disappear, others appear. Pharoah Gary's goal is to determine the correct alignment of the Great Pyramid, to solve the puzzle.

Amazingly, he doesn't get there. I was rooting for an inverted pyramid balanced on its former apex. But Pharoah Gary lays off the throttle at the end and goes with "We may never know."

THE COSMIC GLAND OF MYRNA TOFT: Readings by St. Masterman von Chambray (Underside Press, Appleton, WI, 414 pages, $19.95). Here's a twist on spirit channelling. This is a book that claims to be from another plane of reality, written by one of those goofily-named spirits that get channelled in our world. St. Masterman von Chambray channels Myrna Toft of St. Cloud, MN and she tells him all about pickling and canning, ideas utterly foreign to saints of other planes. But my question is, if this other plane has the word "chambray," can they honestly claim not to know anything about quilting?

ENDS OF THE WORLD—A Guide to Avoiding Apocalyptic Pitfalls by Alise Moran (Wasser's Curl Books, Memphis, TN, 212 pages, $13.95)
THE INFINITE WORLDEATER by Hector Rabin (Crowley Square, Patterson, NJ, 300 pages, $19.95)

Alise Moran has been in contact with multiple timelines of the Earth for several years, and in this work she talks about the connections that have gone dark since December 1998. Given that there are an infinite number of timelines, Moran has come to the conclusion that each of the apocalypses that have befallen alternate Earths have been removed from the realm of possibility for our own Earth. This basic misunderstanding of infinity dims what is otherwise a charming book about how not to be The One/The Anti-Christ/Shiva Incarnate/Trouble Walking/The One Played By The Most Famous Actor In The Movie Version. Given the nature of infinity, there are in fact infinite numbers of alternate Earths where the same exact thing destroys the Earth. That's a riff on Hector Rabin's *THE INFINITE WORLDEATER*, which posits that all apocalypses across all timelines are in fact the same Multi-timeline beast he calls Satan's Coil. Since there are an infinite number of timelines, though, Rabin says that Satan's Coil will be plenty busy until long after humans do themselves in as a species. If you're still unclear on infinity, picture taking a long flight between Moran and Rabin and saying "Oh, so you're a writer?"

A SKEPTIC'S GUIDE TO PARAPSYCHOLOGY by Dr. Yael Oroton (Pill of Worlds, Ocala, FL, 744 pages, $39.95) is like a *PEOPLE* magazine puff interview of Parapsychology Studies, as if they were collectively one pretty, bored celebrity with a movie to shill. It's loaded with hard-hitting questions like "What makes you think that telepathy is centered in the brain," leading to some amazing explanations. It turns out that maybe our livers can actually read other livers, but that it's not terribly relevant if they do. The brain is the boss, after all. Runner-up favorite question: "Does anyone not have psychic abilities?"

THE GOD OF TOUCHDOWNS—

Why Divine Power Cares Who Wins by Turk Whipple (Logos House, Raisin, Arizona, 212 pages, $14.95) If there is a more us vs them version of Christianity than modern sport, it would have to have an astounding body count. This is the usual mix of metaphysical excuses that amounts to God popping up after eating it on his bike and intoning "I meant to do that." Losing teams should pray harder, or accept that God's chosen path for wide receivers will always be more important then any defensive tackle, ever. It's Calvinism with a lottery attached. Who is God's chosen? Find out this Sunday at Lambeau! Note to Christianity: if you're still writing apologia two millennia later, there is no rug big enough to cover that stain.

Are you an immortal hidden among us? Is it getting harder to shift your assets to your new identity every 30 years or so?

New research can help!

Are you one of the Planar Displaced, trapped in this realm in a host body with no financial means? Do you have a Solar Castle with riches piled just out of your reach?

New research can help!

Are you a Child of the Night, trying to reclaim historic lands and property as your true self? Do lawyers run screaming from your presence?

New research can help!

A good, discreet mortal lawyer is just too hard to find. And when you find one, they're gone in the blink of an eye. Face facts: you're going to have to become your own lawyer. The world's entry onto the Information Superhighway has made it easier than ever to file claims without having to risk exposure, staking, or beheading by showing up in a courthouse. With the right knowledge, you can be set for as long as money and property are worshipped as gods. The ***NECROPROBATICON*** is the first addition to Other Knowledge of real estate since the Mad Arab Alhazared's ***NECRONOMICON***. A lot has changed! Send two ingots of silver and a jar of tears to:

Reports From The Seekers

TIRE *gets letters like you can't believe. Seriously. Bags arrived while I was working on this issue. I thought about putting in letters on jitting, but that would mean caring about what Jitters think. It would also mean sifting through a massive amount of mail for context. Various staffers over the years had been collecting letters that inspired or amused them and placed them in folders, which were kept next to a bottle of Wild Turkey in the closet with the water heater. So, here are a few letters from the water heater files.—JIT*

Two From A File Titled "Get A Room"

L. Burdette's rantings on The Star Mariner movement continue to amuse and amaze. At no point has SMm claimed that the universe and all the space between planets was filled with water. This is scurrilous horse apples. There is not nearly enough oxygen in the universe to accomplish this. And if all that water is now gone, what is it now? Steam? L. Burdette's limited understanding of science and his distinctly uncharitable nature prevent him from seeing our assertions clearly.

Simply put, space has always been a vacuum with trace gases and remnants of water bridges between the Star Realms. These water bridges are proven to exist along cosmic key lines, the Stellar Riverbeds. L. Burdette is an intellectual pedophile, preying on people bearing the faith of a child. He should be shunned as a fool and a danger to spiritual children and right-thinking people.

—Oran Kestel, Urania, OH

I read with great interest Oran Kestel's latest broadside against me in this column. I suspect he will submit a letter calling me a spiritual pedophile soon. He used the phrase several times in an otherwise unintelligible rant that he left on my answering machine the other night. His backpedalling dribble about the universe being filled with waterspouts light-years in length is no better than his Universe as Vast Aquarium flummery.

It is a serious failure of critical thinking to suggest cosmic keylines are paths of travel through the universe. The gods that currently use them will sense his heresy soon enough and burn Mr. Kestel alive in his poorly-wired manufactured home. If only the gods read *TIRE*!

—L. Burdette, Urania, OH

There Were Tens Of These

I continue to await publication of my Holy Text in your pages. At an average issue length of 130 pages, surely *TIRE* can muster up a few dozen more pages to bring the LIGHT to the MASSES? What must a deity do in this day and age to bring the WORD?

Zapping stone tablets with lightning counted as publishing, once. These days, if you're not photocopying it, you might as well burn it, for all the people that will see it. IF WE DON'T DO SOMETHING ABOUT THE PROXIMITY OF FIRE AND WATER, WE ARE ALL DOOMED!

Two new elements must be discovered and put in use immediately! I have already added Steam (Air/Water), Charcoal (Earth/Fire), Flamethrowers (Fire/Water), and Mud (Earth/Water), but the spots between Earth and Air, and Fire and Air remain elusive. Dust storms? Furnaces? HVAC?

Without followers and scholars of this important work, THE WORLD IS DOOMED! All liquid will explode on January 12, 1985! The clock is ticking! Your toilet will no longer be your friend, that happy hole in your house that takes the waste away. It is a long fuse, attached to the ocean, waiting to go off!

—Langtry Dean, Satanta, KS

GHOSTBUSTERS Is Not A Documentary, People!

Just a quick note on spirit traps from your October issue. Looking into them will not hurt you. That damn GHOSTBUSTERS movie is spreading misinformation. Perception is the medium through which spirits become as real as they're going to be on this plane. If you look away before the trap closes, you'll have one pissed off and

slightly wiser spectre on your hands.

—W. Arganbright, Francisco, CO

Look What I Found

I am writing again to ask that you either stop writing about me, or start paying me for the privilege. I'm a private citizen, seeking no fame or notoriety, at least not for any of this. Ought we not have a choice in our futures? Are you so committed to a destiny where you are the only people with a choice in my life?

If you are the deciders of my fate, choose something better for me than this. I look at a crowd and wonder which of them wants to steal my hair. My life is a strategy game full of pitfalls, or a role-playing game where someone else rolled me up and chose my class.

You've been telling the world for years that I peaked at age nine. That's paralyzing. Some nights I can't breathe, thinking about the offices of *TIRE*, how you keep my life in a plastic bucket that you routinely piss in to bump up your circulation. You don't insult or malign me, but you praise me. Your lawyers insist this means there is no libel. Is there anything more damning than being called a former prophet? It's like being called a lapsed facist, or an unemployed executioner. All it does is raise the kind of questions that nobody else has to answer about themselves.

In your March 1988 issue, you announced to the world that I'd changed my major from Pre-Law to Philosophy. That was how my folks found out about it. Thanks loads.

Originally I'd been attracted to it because of symbolic logic, but now I have a new reason to dig deep into the wisdom about the world. I am going to aggressively debunk this JIT business. I'm going to take every notion that went into making that damn drawing and explode it. I dare you not to publish it. I DARE YOU. I'm arming up for philosophical battle. Get ready.

—J. I. Thomas, Lubbock, TX

[This was in a folder with every other broadside I sent this place in college. There are marks indicating that their lawyers had reviewed them. None ever saw print. I really thought they would publish at least one and try to mock it, at least. But it wasn't preceeded with the secret handshake or knowing nod that made this approved JIT material.]

The Short Answer Is No

With the coming planetary alignment, will *TIRE* have any features exploring its significance? It's less of an event than the Harmonic Convergence, astronomically. The planets and houses don't match up in any significant way, but the first thing you learn when you look for your fate in the stars is that the moment you think nothing special is happening, SOMETHING SPECIAL IS HAPPENING.

It's like watching a soap opera every day. The one day you think you can miss it, something huge happens. Really, soaps have a lot of moving parts. While you're immersed in one, time seems to slow down. Lots of little things are in motion, but you can only appreciate that aspect from the outside. If you listen to a description of one episode, it sounds amazing. Lots of things happen. Much information is imparted. But those events are done by then. More events are already in motion. I view the Universe the same way, and look forward to the wisdom of the stars, however it chooses to enter me.

—E. Taso, Winnetka, IL

Add "In Bed" To These

In four dimensions, a pyramid is an infinite pointed streak traveling through the universe, looking for its other end.

In four dimensions, money is nothing but space, punctuated by empty things.

In four dimensions, love beats like a heart that disappears when it contracts.

In four dimensions, time will tell.

—L. Barnard, Bartlesville, OK

But A Metaphor For What?

Dear *TIRE*. You'll never guess what happened to me. I was minding my own business in the Second Airlock at my local Church of Christ, Astronaut. I was meditating on the sound not made in space. Then in comes the Personification of the Stellar Advent, wearing only the thinnest wisp of Doubt. She gave me a look like she meant business.

Did she ever!

That little bit of Doubt she was wearing slid down my face and down my chest and under my ribcage, swirling around my bowels, looking for my Phreen. I gazed up at her and

114

she was, without a doubt, here to elevate me.

I tried to rise, Doubt swirling in my guts. She laid an appendage on my face and cooed "You can't elevate yourself, cadet. Let me elevate you." She then made the Sign of Schirra, which slid into my face like a key into a lock. The next thing I know, I'm looking at my own neck, my chin below me. My face had fallen forward, like it was on a hinge, and I was looking up at my head!

I waited for the Personification to reach in, but instead, she brought in her friend, the Apolline Sigil. Even without appendages, he drifted toward me and rooted through my brains like they were bills in a mailbox. It took only a second to erupt into a Third Elevation. I felt like a teenager!

Landing spent on the wisp of Doubt (how did it get out of my bowels?), I started to meditate on the journey, but they wanted more. Needless to say, nobody slept that night! My bowels are still sore!

—Cadet R. Bowman (CoCA),
Ruidoso, NM

Attempting To Hurt Ruth's Feelings Is Futile, Guys.

Let this serve as our resignation from *TIRE*, before it reverts back into the organ of a repressive Old Age worldview. It is a devolution we cannot bear to witness. Many of us have devoted decades to bringing the truth to seekers under *TIRE*'s aegis, and to have you declare that the New Age is here (in the pages of *TIRE* itself!) is a deception of the highest

magnitude. That you would involve the JIT in this insult may be the worst crime of all! We will not participate in the burial of the magazine we love. If the JIT wishes his revenge, he will have to do it all himself!

—The True Seekers of *TIRE*

[The news of the advent of the New Age had preceeded my arrival at the TIRE *offices. What the staff hadn't been told was that the JIT was to be the Guest Editor of this issue. I was their pink slip from Ruth, I think. When the JIT shows up and blows the whistle, that crowd knows the game's over. Most of them packed their stuff and left without a word. A few huddled up, wrote the above letter, and then split. I had to actually fire the ad guys. They weren't subtle people.]*

Finally, A Bit Of Business

Still have not received my Wheel of Karma bonus for upping to the lifetime subscription. Punishment decisions are very hard to make in the close cases, and my need for the Wheel of Karma increases every day. My practice world is beginning to fall apart without it.

My fuzzy worshippers worship me not at all ever since I blew the Senior Mittens/Junior Mittens naming decision. They sense that there may be no guiding principle at all in my Godhood. It may well be that I am not at all cut out to be a figure of worship.

Anyway, please send the Wheel as soon as you can. I may yet be a legendary hero to these creatures.

—Morgan LePeer, St. Cloud, MN

METER ANGELS ARE REAL

A red-faced meter maid in Half Mile, MT is now admitting that meter angels might be real after all. "When the city installed three meters in front of the courthouse last year, everything seemed normal," says JoLinda Kettlebaum. "It was mostly to keep folks from storing their car in the visitor spots for the winter." But it was someone with winter storage on the brain that had a different idea about parking turnover.

"We noticed that in December, we weren't issuing any tickets. Plus the meters were filling up a lot faster than usual," explains Kettlebaum. "It was a real mystery." The trail led to a nearby donation pail for the Salvation Army, and up the tree next to it. "Nuts were falling from the tree into the pail," explains bell-ringer Ethan Scovill. "I saw the squirrel jump in and get them. I didn't think it was taking change too."

An inspection of the tree revealed twenty dollars in assorted change. Patient observation of the tree revealed another squirrel regularly taking change from the tree and feeding the meters. "The squirrel saw people put their change in the little trees, so to speak," says local animal behaviorist Dr. Alaine Sanchez (Cat.D.). "So it cleaned its own house by helping humans store their change. It's just good neighbors."

[*The original AP news story includes the following graf, crossed out on the* TIRE *copy.—JIT*] The Salvation Army, however, does not share this rosy assessment. "These squirrels are stealing from the poor," says bell-ringer Ethan Scovill. "I don't find that as cute as some folks." Scovill has been issued a seasonal concealed-carry gun permit for this and future holiday seasons. "This is to protect Christmas for the poor humans victimized by these squirrels." To date, Scovill has not managed to stop them. "They may be meter angels to you, but I don't own a car."

Jitting for Fun and Prophet

The creation of the work that came to be called *MEGACON-TEMPLATIONS* was deceptively simple. There was no preparation, no ritual to it. It was the second day of a comic book convention in sunny Florida, at which I nearly froze my balls off the day before. My table was in Artist Alley, right under a massive air handler.

I'd purchased an overpriced but very smart Godzilla hoodie late on the first day, and it seemed that I might just survive the experience. Strolling from the hotel to the convention, I took a path along a hedge and was confronted with a Walgreens. I did not hesitate. I did not break my stride. I went straight inside to the school supply aisle and the tools seemed to choose themselves.

Crayons, not markers. Rough drawing paper seemed correct. I had paid and was back out the door before I'd decoded this activity. I would draw the God of the King once more. I would take aim at the mindset of the nine year old and see what was going on in there.

The first image I drew was not of the God of the King. Now there was the lion of the God. There was no capitalization for "lion." I was already farther away from the original notion than before.

The story included three grey kings, only one of which survived the story. The action spread across multiple planes, multiple worlds, and included some uncomfortable looking hats. As I wrote and drew, people would approach my table. The act of drawing often lures people close. When they saw what I was drawing, they often made a yuck face and wandered on. Sometimes kids wanted to draw with me. But this was serious business.

I was accused a couple of times of mocking talented artists by engaging in this behavior at a comic book convention. I told them I was drawing at the top of my ability. I could certainly draw worse. I don't know if any Jitters saw me there. Noone seemed interested in me in that way there.

The next year, when I was selling the results of the previous year's work, a woman asked me about it. She asked me if I knew the mysteries. I played dumb and asked if she meant the Eleusinian Mysteries. She started to explain it to me. I had actually met a Jitter who didn't know who I was!

After a bit of back and forth, I stuck out my hand and introduced myself. Holding my hand quietly for a moment, the realization nearly crushed her. Still gripping my hand, she backed away from me, saying "I think I have to get away from you." I extracted my hand and went back to not selling my book.

Not one Jitter has bought that book. I kept it out of Books In Print just so I could look every single person who bought it in the eye. It turned out to be a not lot of eyes. Even with a book full of jitting from the source, I couldn't draw these people into the open.

That didn't stop *TIRE* from talking about it, though. Story after story appeared about revelations in the book. They weren't guessing. They had read it. They never printed any of the images, because a "c" in a circle is more powerful than a pentagram, even to these people.

It was the last time I tried to profit from my status as the JIT's inspiration. Now that *TIRE* is history, I figure that's it. Arthur Peyton Corley and his ilk figured out how to monetize jitting, and I didn't. But, according to the rule of three, that means the next guy to try it will be the one that makes a million dollars. It's usually the third guy that does it.

Like the man says: "The wind would prove only one of them right." This is a fact of my life. Even if it all died down today, the results of it would persist. I have steely-eyed dedicated fans that seem to want nothing from me, but who stand ready just in case they might later. Am I a spiritual backup plan? A figure to believe in for no other reason than I might have another epiphany? I'm an empty wine vessel, held for the day when I might suddenly be refilled from within.

I don't even get to be a has-been prophet. People in every field get to coast on their former glories, but religious figures are either holy or they're dogshit. The donut shops are staffed by yogis. Wal-Mart has a storeroom full of seers. Vessels for beings from Other Planes are delivering ten dollar handies behind strip malls. And this jitting wunderkind is making comic books.

Maybe a better comparison is the aging child star, whose chipmunk cheeks look troubling on an adult face. There is that frantic search for a second life that usually preceeds the report of their surrender to the rules of the world. I want to be free of it, but there is a charm to being saddled with it. It's like claiming there's nobility in poverty. The coping becomes comfortable, and is missed when the pain that it eased is finally gone.

There is a lot of talk about Y2K, and all the world-ending horrors it holds. With the demise of the source of my pain, the world has indeed changed for me. This process of pissing on its grave has been a funeral for the JIT. The Internet will absorb some of it, but the real-world component is the fuel for this faith. The rest will be copied and knocked off and I will be forgotten.

Then someone will make a ton of cash on it and I'll shake my fist at the whole thing and say "I was a prophet once. Seriously. I was nine . . . ."

—John Ira Thomas

CLASSIFIED ADVERTISING

TIRE magazine accepts Classified Advertising for this section, reserving the right to exclude any advertising that does not conform to its standards. Rates are $1 per word, one-time; $.92 per word, 3-times; $.87 per word, 6-times; $.82 per word, 12-times. Address is free, as long as it conforms to U. S. Post Office norms. *[There's no way in hell that I'm going to let these people rob anyone with my help. As a result, I've blacked out all the addresses. The addresses were free in the first place, so that's the way it goes, seekers.—JIT]*

TOMES-GUIDES

They're not taking volunteers to be the Antichrist, but there are loads of problematic philosophies looking for the right mortal to be their foe! Know what it takes to be THE ENEMY! $15 for mailing list, general requirements for infernal roles across multiple creeds and societies. ███████, NY, NY 10029.

The contents of your used Kleenex hold future-revealing patterns more accurate than tea leaves! Learn to read them! Send $20 for book, mucus color chart. BLOWING THE FUTURE, ██████████, Esdale, WY 82648.

THE NEW TESTAMENT WAS VOLUME 2. Volume nine is now available! The Nicene Council has been back in business since 1846, working tirelessly to bring the COMPLETE Gospel to the world! You've only been doing part of the work of Christianity and making your mortal life a passport to Heaven if you've only read the first two volumes. Without knowledge of the Gospels of Hector and The Mole Men, your chances of being Hellbound increase dramatically! The Holy Press of the Nicene Council, ██████████████, Baylich, NJ 08005.

PRE-FREUDIAN DREAM ANALYSIS. Get the penises and vaginas out of dream interpretation! Our unconscious isn't a naughty Mad-Lib! It has information to impart! THE PRE-FREUDIAN DREAM CATALOG starts with the work of Artemidoros Daldianus and helps update other ancient dream catalogs to get at the modern meaning clouded by maniacs who spend all day thinking about their bits and parts. Send $30 to Pillar and Stones Press, ████████████████, Cooter, OR 97031.

SPIRITUAL IQ TESTING! Even if the spirit you channel is who it says it is, does it really know anything? Has it interpreted the data at its end accurately? Learn to give IQ tests to the spirits beyond the veil and save valuable time for cultivating a relationship with a spirit that really knows what it's doing. Workbook $10. Special Testing Service, █████████████, Benlow, MD 21561.

TRICK YOURSELF INTO BEING RICH! Do you seem to fail no matter what you do? Harness that power with autohypnotic techniques and flip the switch on your life! If your subconscious has a perfect streak of failure at life, finances, love, then retrain it to think that being healthy, rich, and fully satisfied in the bedroom are failures! Your subconscious will go right to work, thinking it's making your life a living hell with a high-paying job, robust health, and pretty ladies. Send $30 for THE ENEMY IN YOUR MIDBRAIN by Spencer Cleland. Psychic Judo Press, ██████████████, Relic, NM 88344.

ASTROLOGY

LEARN ASTROLOGICAL SHORTHAND! A full chart can take days to fully delineate. Save time and ink, with no loss of content and meaning! Only someone who knows shorthand can read Asterisk, so you can spend your time where it counts—imparting the wisdom of the stars to your clients! They're not paying to watch you draw a chart. They want answers! Learn Asterisk at no risk today! FREE STARTER COURSE! Send SASE to ASTERISK, ████████, Downers Grove, IL 60515.

ALTERNATE TIMELINE CHARTS! See what the stars hold for a version of you, just one universe over! Multiple-timeline charts can be cross-referenced to weed out false positives and weak connectors that make for poor choices. First timeline chart is FREE! Discounts available for bundling timelines by health, fame, power, sex appeal. RIGID DESIGNATOR, ███████████, Bad Axe, MI 48413.

SPACE DEBRIS AFFECTS YOU! It's scientifically established that the stars exert subtle yet powerful control of our lives. New research indicates that derelict satellites of a certain size, especially ones with nuclear fuel, can affect us nearly as much as the stars! Their closeness to all of us, whirling over our heads, gives them great power over our love, investments, and the quality of our enemies! Near-Earth Derelict Atlas $50, readings $25. AT THE FEET OF STARS, ███████, Purdymouth, WV 26351.

BIOFEEDBACK

DID YOU KNOW that Thought is a particle as well as a wave? It makes sense! We are, of course, beings of Pure Light! Learn the secrets of Biofeedback from an Einsteinian approach! Start with a $10 Particle Biofeedback chart! The transitions in our lives are not always smooth, like a wave on a conventional Biofeedback chart. Thought Teleportation is no longer an unproven phenomenon! Einsteinian Academy of Thought, ██████████, Berkeley, CA 94704.

BUSINESS OPPORTUNITIES

MAKE MONEY WRITING SENTENCES! I may have purchased an ad to tell you this, but someone's going to send me the $40 this ad costs to find out why. Maybe two people will do it. LEARN MY SECRET! Send $40 to The Writing Well, ████████, Chicago, IL 60602.

SEARCHING FOR ANSWERS? They don't always help. Be the one writing the questions! That's where the power is. The answers may come someday, but until then send $5 to learn how to take control of...THE QUESTIONS, ███████, Dubuque, IA 52001.

THIMBLES! I just told you an important business secret for FREE! Send me SASE, and I'll tell you what it means for you, your family, and your financial security for decades to come! FINGERHELMET, ████████████, Mallopont, WI 54491.

DIDN'T GET YOUR ITEM? Remember to include your FULL address when writing to any of our fine advertisers. Many have told us that they get loads of returned mail because of incomplete addresses. Think of all that wisdom not reaching all those seekers! Clearly PRINT your name, address, city, state, and zip. And don't forget to tell them that you "saw it in *TIRE*!"

100 HIGH-PAYING JOBS NO-ONE WANTS that can yield big returns to the right people! Details, letter drop locations $5. CS-12-R, ██████████, Old Ulm, WV 25917.

LEARN TO MAKE BENEDICTINE AT HOME! Starter kit with recipe, habit, and Papal Encouragement Writ from the Holy Father in Rome only $1500! Serious inquiries only. OUR LADY OF SWAYING, ██████████, Rome, GA 30161.

SECRET LAW TRANSFERS DEBTS to dead people! Learn the secrets used only by immortals among us! To them, it's just a normal part of financial housekeeping. To you, it can be the key to living a mortal life to the fullest! Lifeplan, ██████████, Gornick, RI 02816.

BE THE KING OF MANY DOMAINS! Addresses on the Information Superhighway are still being claimed. Many big businesses and public entities don't own their own addresses in the virtual world to come. Wouldn't you like to be their landlord? For $50 an address, you can start your path to financial independence! Your first test is to decode this address—admin@██████████████.com —if you know how to contact us with only this information, you are ready!

HEALTH-BEAUTY

PRODUCE LESS WASTE! Learn the secrets of retaining number 2! The bulk of our solid waste is dead stomach bacteria and water. Every living thing is committed to this offloading of important elements as if it can never change. Most people even believe it's healthy! New Gut-Bac Formula vastly increases the life of your alimentary bacteria. Once the lifespan of this bacteria is extended, it can be trained to break down items previously thought impossible to digest! Nine easy-to-swallow pills a day will change your life! Write for full catalog, testimonials. Retention Laboratories, ████████████████, Pottsdam, MS 38864.

LOST HAIR CAN BE FOUND AGAIN! Don't believe charlatans who move follicles around and insist it's "your hair." Your original hair went somewhere, and we can find it! Once located, we can run sophisticated tests to see if reimplantation is possible. It has worked in a majority of our cases! We don't work miracles. We're just psychic scientists and detectives with a dream of a full head of YOUR hair, for you. Send lock of current hair and $50 for consultation. HAIR TODAY, ███ ████████████, Yeager, ME 04490.

ALLERGIES GOT YOU DOWN? Nasally-fitted poultices are the answer! These small, sterile bags slip easily into each nostril where they comfortably rest on nasal membranes inflamed by allergens. After a few breathing exercises, you won't even notice they're there! Enjoy the outdoors again! You can finally get that pet! Embrace nasal freedom! $25 for nasal sizer, allergy checklist (with test samples), breathing exercise pamphlet. Cost of poultices based on cavity size, severity of allergies. RECLAIM THE OUTDOORS, ███ ████████, Forest Ridge, MT 59464.

INSTRUCTION

THERE IS PSYCHIC PARENTHESIS WAITING FOR YOU. Learn to read the asides in others' scripts! Only they know for now, but you can know what they're saying to The Quiet Audience! Get on the inside of human behavior and motivation! Exercises, quizzes, helmet included. Sample $5. Steve Podharsleigh, ███████████████, Temecula, CA 92590.

SEEK THE ANALJESUS! Colonic seances, Berend treatments. PEOPLE IN YOUR COLON HAVE LIVED BEFORE! Video, booklet, tubing $35. Rectalgeist Institute, ████████████████, Los Renales, CA 95939.

THREE KINDS OF ESP ARE TEACHABLE, but two are fatal! Don't make the mistake R. Krasnoyich made in Tunguska 6/30/1908! Your neighbors don't have to pay the price for your ascension! Send $3 for sample lesson. ████████, Needles, CA 92363.

PROGRAM YOUR DREAM SCHEDULE! Former TV Executive explains the secrets to Must See Dreaming! Timeslot Institute, ███ ████████, Century City, CA 90025.

DOES LEARNING WHILE ASLEEP LEAVE YOU TIRED and distracted the next day? Don't study all night! Learn the art of Speed Listening! It'll be the last thing you need to learn while you're awake! $40 for book and high-speed tape player. Nocturnal Cramming, ████████, Lexington, KY 40507.

OTHERS POSSESS SPECIAL POWERS and don't know it! Why awaken them? Do you trust them? Learn to harness untapped power in others! You'll be powerful, and no-one will be the wiser! It's the one with the power that they come for in the end. $10 for first 2 lessons. PSYCHIC GRACKLING, ████████, Los Angeles, CA 91754.

WE KNOW ABOUT LIFE after Death, but what about the Death that comes after Life after Death? Send SASE and five stamps to SECOND DEATH, ████████, Ellis, IL 61483.

PYROKINESIS IS REAL! One in five people have the ability, but only one in a million can start a fire. The bulk of pyrokinetics, with training, can brown a piece of toast with only the power of their mind and our patent-pending Pyrokinesis Focus Plate. The plate is FREE with purchase of our 10 CD set to teach you how to harness the fire inside you! 10 CD set and plate are $79.95 with FREE SHIPPING. THE FIRE INSIDE, ████████, Piedmar, TN 37755.

THERE ARE NO MASONIC DEGREES above 32nd, but there are six before the first! Send SASE and any coupons for dog food to SIX DEGREES BELOW, ████████, Trobring, WA 98532.

ADVERTISE IN TIRE and get the word out about your product! SEEKERS READ TIRE!

122

MISCELLANEOUS

CONCEPTS too large for the brain to handle! Pamphlet, cerebral truss, $6. Herniated Consciousness, ██████, Denver, CO 80012.

PSYCHIC? Already know what's up? Then subscribe to OLD NEWS, the monthly magazine for PSYCHICS ONLY! It arrives in shreds because you already know what's in it! Leave it on the coffee table to impress friends! Single issue $10, 1-year subscription $100. OLD NEWS, ██████████, Fellowes, SC 29014.

I WANT nothing to do with you. Do NOT send $1 to NOBODY, ██████████, Sapling, VT 05077.

SPEAK DIRECTLY to the founding fathers! Channelling the great men who created the greatest nation on earth is the only path away from the New World Order! Hear the authoritative voices of the men who forged a nation! They see what's happening to America and want to help! What does Abraham Baldwin think of waiting periods? Would John Langdon approve of a rape exception? Would Richard Dobbs Spaight belong to a modern militia? Send $10 for receptivity test to see which founding father wants to speak through you! The Channelled Constitutional Congress will be in July, as always, at the VFW in Foley, PA! THE FOUND FATHERS, ██████████, Foley, PA 17545.

HANDWRITING ANALYSIS! Every stroke of the pen tells your life story! Make a J now. Do you see your love life there? We can help! Curve chart and spiral pen attachment to change your life by changing your writing! $25 to POWERSTROKE, ██████, Irving, DE 19947.

LEARN SPRITIUAL MARIMBA! Play the great gospel classics on the marimba! Easy to learn, haunting results. Make a special place for yourself in any congregation! Marimba, course, charts for 50 popular sacred hymns $100. SUCCESS GUARANTEED! Ross Mail-Order Marimba Seminary, Our Lady of the Perpetual, ██████████, Reedtree, FL 31634.

METAL DETECTORS

YOU MAY LOOK FOR GOLD, but you will not find it here. You need to be out in the world with your R420 Maxscan Mk II, looking for the find that will change your life! Metal detectors can't find gold or silver. You need something that finds what you want! Nine settings, including Gold, Silver, Coins, Liquor, Papyrus, and Love! Unit and instruction booklet $99.95. El Dorado Instruments, ██████, Lampasas, TX 76550.

MONEY-MAKING OPPORTUNITIES

BANNED IN SEVEN STATES—how to make money flipping pet real estate. One percent of all inherited land went to cats last year. Learn the secrets of animal to human real estate transfer from America's biggest feline landowner and make big bucks! Instructive book, plus listings in your area, $25. Write Princess Fancyfeet, ██████████, NY, NY 10036.

I GET PAID FOR GETTING PAID. Learn the secret to profiting off of your own financial transactions! Send for particulars. X-242-R, ██████████, Chicago, IL 60610.

MAKE MONEY OPENING BOXES! Intensely disliked public figure seeks screeners for large volume of mail. ANONYMOUS, ██████████, NY, NY 11222.

WANT BIG BUCKS? Get smarter! How do you get smarter? Send $10 to Ima Sukor, ██████████, Barnum, OH 44883.

TAXES ARE FOR PEOPLE WHO PAY TAXES. Learn how not to! $10 to FREEDOM, ██████, North Side, Cayman Islands.

THE IRS IS SLOW and stupid! They can be held off forever with the right strategies. $10 to FREEDOM, ██████, North Side, Cayman Islands

MAKE MONEY OPENING MAIL! Just open it and drop in prepaid envelopes back in the mail. WORK FROM HOME! FREEDOM, ██████, North Side, Cayman Islands.

123

ORGANIZATIONS

THE SECOND CHURCH OF CHRIST, VAMPIRE is now Harvest Life Church! We welcome all red-blooded mortal Americans who wish to be washed in the Blood of Christ and help practice Abundant Living! Send for free pamphlet. Harvest Life, ██████████, New Orleans, LA 70112.

YOU READ ABOUT EVIL organizations trying to take over the world, but nobody ever asks you to join. Do they really exist? OF COURSE THEY DO! But they don't put classified ads in *TIRE*, because they have standards. There's no room for sloppy unfocused thinkers in a secret organization out to enslave humanity. They'll make exceptions for people who make astounding breakthroughs in knowledge that can be leveraged (or for their near and dear). But unless you are some kind of genius (or someone a genius loves), that's not your path. We're not looking for walk-ons either. We just wanted you to know that you're unworthy. We are an EVIL ORGANIZATION. No, you can't have our address. Set $10 on fire, because we told you to.

PERSONAL

I WILL TELL YOU YOUR DREAMS! Don't remember your dreams? I can help recover those memories! Send $5 plus SASE for questionnaire. Reasonable rates for multiple readings. AWAKE! ██████████, Arshin, MO 65075.

PERHAPS YOU'VE ALREADY BEEN hypnotized and this is the phrase that activates you! Each full moon, every person who gazes upon it is hypnotised! The message is clear: ascend! All you need is to read the activation phrase to begin! Do you see it here? You will know what to send to ACTIVATED, ██████████, Peqin, WA 98022.

TWO QUESTIONS ANSWERED, one yes, the other no. Send $3 for more. QUEStions, ██████████, Tempe, AZ 85281.

BUTTON READER CAN HELP YOU! Snip one button off used clothing and send with $5 to Bettina, ██████████, Agelthorp, KS 67428.

I WILL JIT FOR YOU! Do you lack artistic ability? Or has illness degraded your fine motor skills? I CAN HELP! I focus on items and details from your life and enter a transpersonal living trance state. I BECOME YOU AND THEN I JIT! It's your jitting, for I can become you! Send SASE for free list of items and personal details required. I JIT FOR YOU, ██████████, Purley, WV 26155.

POTSHERDS CAN HELP YOU travel through time! Archaeologists have been glum about finding pounds and tons of broken pots where the ancients once lived. But these items were personal to those who used them. They bear resonances that can be channelled and questioned via an experienced medium! Which medium? YOU! Send $25 for starter potsherd and guide to channelling. POTS! ██████████, Vagabond, OR 97751.

SECRET POWER OF FUTURE MASTERS is calling back to you! $10, as long as you promise not to tell anyone else. SPOFM, ██████████, Castellero, CO 81201.

THROWING AWAY your nail clippings? Why not just throw your hard-earned money out with it? We pay by the tablespoon! We are not making clones. Genetechnic Labs, ██████████, Cambridge, MA 02139.

PRODUCTS-NOVELTIES

REvolution! Get a do-over for the last million years! Do you want a lighter, aerodynamic frame? A brain made larger by thinking instead of throwing? A tail? Details, cream samples. $10 REvolute! ██████████, Wilattit, MD 21157.

IF YOU'VE MADE YOUR SOUL GROW, it's time for the next challenge...growing a new soul! Souls wear out. Life is hard sometimes. Be ready to move on with a pristine new soul when the time is right! CD, planter, soil guide, $45. SOULSEED, ██████████, Atchison, KS 66002.

PSYCHOPHOTONIC CAPACITOR. Store your psychic power for when you need it most! Grenades available. Plans $15, Finished unit $350. LIGHTMIND, ██████████, Potts, WY 82442.

THE SPHERE IS THE WRONG shape for crystal gazing! Forget Crystal Balls! Learn the power of the Crystal Shaft! Send $3 for catalog and free grip chart. FUTURE SHAFT, ████████████, Phoenix, AZ 85003.

STERILE REUSABLE MOTES! Apply and remove sterile, washable, reusable mote from your eye to gain revelation! What will happen when you remove the mote? When you're ready, try the beam! Starter Mote Kit $20. Master George, ████████, Turnley, TX 76842.

TAPES-CDs

SHORDEN MISE has at last gotten permission to share the full knowledge of the cosmos! She is busy recording the complete knowledge, but you can start now! Box 1 contains 300 minutes on quanta, fanta, sublimita, and all the particles yet to be discovered by the atom-smashers! Learn to spot subtle frequencies and particle wobbles in your environment! Box 2, "Dirt, Water, Love, and Stone," focuses on the elements made from the essential particles. Boxes are $199. Order today! You don't want to get left behind when Box 100 is released! Full knowledge means unaided stellar travel! AT LAST THE TRUTH, ████████, Panoply, AZ 86032.

LEARN COMPLETE HEARING! Have you ever been told that someone was calling out to you and you didn't hear it? We all have! That's because hearing is selective. Learn to absorb the full range of sound and have your ears work the way your eyes do! Get the whole picture! Send for informative CD, $25. TOTAL HEARING, ████████████, Gallanghen, NE 69152.

RANDOM ACCESS WISDOM! Divination with your microwave oven is now possible! CD with random words, baked in a microwave for less than a second, will randomly track, giving multidimensional entities a chance to speak their wisdom through a process seemingly goverened by chance! It's not easy. Too long and the CD will spark and become useless. 3 CDs and instructions, $25. More CDs available in bulk. NUKED KNOWLEDGE, ████████, Langeia, IL 61910.

ARE BLANK TAPES REALLY BLANK? Just because you hear nothing, doesn't mean nothing is there. There may be no sound, but there is video! Successful conspiracy has prevented video capability on cassette decks, until now! Furimata Incorp's suppressed technology can now be yours! Tape deck $1000, screens in a variety of sizes and resolutions. Write for FREE catalog. Hank's Audio/Video, ████████, Los Angeles, CA 90068.

RELIGION

DO WE HAVE ALL OF THE COMMANDMENTS? For the surprising answer, write: THOU SHALT NOT, ████████, Fenly, AL 35950.

FAITH DIAPERS! Make a love offering for one and your baby's offering will bring good luck! Possibly fame, fortune, good looks? Who would deny these to their child? Faith Diaper Ministry, ████████, Tallahasse, FL 32301.

LEARN THE SECRETS of the Heliand! This late translation of the gospel for the Saxons holds key knowledge not in the New Testament text! What does Odin know that Jesus doesn't? OAKEN TRUTHS, ████████, Minneapolis, MN 55404.

ORDINATION IS A FORMALITY! A piece of paper that confers power is nothing but an amulet and therefore WITCHCRAFT! Thousands of well-meaning preachers are selling you tainted Word! Conspiracy exposed! De-Vestment, ████████, Pooley, OH 45634.

THE HOLY WORD WILL DISAPPEAR from the Earth on November 1, 2000! No copies will be spared! Angels gave John Smith only a few years with their Holy Text, and we got 2000 years! Our only hope is Fahrenheit 451 type memorization and retranscription when the Holy Word can once again be transmitted by the pen! Many books still open for memorization (esp. Chronicles). SAVE THE BIBLE, ████████████, Mackwon, ID 83226.

SEEKERS BUY what they see in TIRE!

SCIENTIFIC BREAKTHROUGH

PISS IS HOMEOPATHIC MAN! Shocked? The truth is $5! G. Gaines, ▉▉▉▉▉, Smyrna, GA 30080.

THERE ARE THREE ELEMENTS lighter than hydrogen. Scientists engaged in conspiracy to suppress this knowledge! Send $5 for pamphlet, conclusive proof. Three Squares Back, ▉▉▉▉▉, Pasadena, CA 91101.

THE PYRAMIDS ARE SQUARE at the base! Startling geometric discovery invalidates Pyramid Power! Geometricians in India have located the TRUE source of power at Giza! New pendants yield results! Send $3 for catalog. PYRAMID SQUARED, ▉▉▉▉▉ ▉▉▉▉, Seamilk, FL 32692.

RICH? IMPOTENT? New knowledge about the monkey's paw can flip the two, making you virile and frugal! Instructions, including the runaway bestseller 500 Ways To Live On Less Than Nothing by S. Harper, $500. Romany Hall of Research, ▉▉▉▉▉▉, Downstate, NY 12723.

THE METAL WE KNOW as gold is in fact blue! Subtle changes to the atmosphere since Hiroshima have resulted in a change in the way light reflects off of element Au! The government, believing gold spoilage had occurred, dumped the contents of Fort Knox into nearby abyssals to hide what they thought was an embarrassing failure to keep gold fresh! Funds needed for salvage mission. It may be blue, but it's real gold! We have to save the world economy from collapse! Prospectus, postage-paid envelope to send your contribution available. OPERATION GOLDSAVE, ▉▉▉▉, Hazelwort, VA 22971.

SELF-IMPROVEMENT

SUCCESS IS A FREQUENCY! Learn to tune your senses to pick up the signal! All the information on successful behavior is transmitted from every living thing to every other living thing. Ants know it. Look how well they work together! You can know it too! Quit second-guessing your behavior! Send $10 to MANTENNA, ▉▉▉▉▉▉▉, Hedrach, ND 58357.

HOW CAN I FIND and harness the power of the second prostate? Impress the ladies! Second Wind Pharmaceuticals, ▉▉▉▉▉▉, Lawrence, KS 66044.

BELIEF IS EASY, but can it be easier? Do you find that when presented with truths you are at first skeptical? Do you feel foolish when you realize the truth was right all along? As we age, we find ourselves growing ever more skeptical, insulating us from the truth! Learn to trust your instinct to believe! Send $20 to LEARNING TRUST, ▉▉▉▉▉, Kopley, AZ 86046.

YOUR PINKY CAN BE A THUMB! Evolution says that certain traits are selected to travel on up the evolutionary ladder. Some we cannot control. Some traits we hide. Some we can develop and pass on! Special exercises and bindings can change your useless pinky into a functional thumb. Think of the grip you'll have! $30 for kit. EVOLVE! ▉▉▉▉▉▉, Onlsow, LA 71355.

SERVICES

KEEP GETTING YOUR MAIL when the inevitable comes. We will adjust your latitude/longitude coordinates when earth axis shift occurs. Address changes also possible. Send $25 to POLE WATCH, ▉▉▉▉▉▉, East Liberty, IA 52576.

MY DOG KNOWS THINGS. He found a lost girl, and he can find someone for you! Fees are flexible, but be careful what you ask, as he is not allowed out of the yard anymore. Tell my dog what you're looking for and receive a FREE consultation and estimate for finding what you've lost! Send your question and a sample of your scent to "Menachem" BACON, ▉▉▉▉▉▉, Slapout, OK 73848.

MANUSCRIPT "REJECTED" AGAIN? Almost every famous novel was rejected dozens of times before being accepted. Many authors spend years in this awful and grueling process. We take the work out of mass rejection! It's going to happen anyway, so why not let us take care of the mailing, the waiting, the reading of the rejection letters? Packages start out at 10 rejections for $500. DEAR SIR OR MADAM, ▉▉▉▉▉▉, NY, NY 11233.

126

CHECKER READINGS can tell you more than any star chart! Simply log the moves in a game of checkers you play with anyone and we use the positions and patterns to diagnose your weak points and opportunities for improvement! Send $10 for checker chart and instructions for first reading to KING ME, ████████, Rocklord, SD 57345.

STUDY COURSES

HOW WELL DO YOU KNOW YOURSELF? Are you living a second life while you sleep? Do you have a dream lover and a dream house in the suburbs? If it's a better life for you, then it's time to trade places! Make your dream reality happen! Your dreams may become as boring as your current life, but you'll need the rest from living your joy all day long! Somatic charts, list of sacrifices required only $50! DreamSwap, █████, Hurlburt, SC 29556.

GET THE DEGREE YOU NEED! B.P.A.s available in Applied Metaphysics, Multi-Planar Calculus, Astral Body Pathology, Pattern Manipulation, Hidden Organ Revelation, and many more! No transcripts required! Send $2 for course catalog. The Ivy Scholarly Academy of Real Knowledge, ██████████, Cambridge, MA 02139.

ARE YOU USING YOUR JOINTS correctly? Just as breathing is relearned in the Shaolin tradition, so too we must consider and reinvent the way in which we use our joints. We have been slaves to instinct, assuming that knuckles and knees only go one direction. Learn the secrets of human worms and eastern contortionists! Send $10 for one simple lesson to show you the truth. KNUCKLE UP, ████████, Oppley, MI 49730.

LEARN ANIMAL REPAIR! Veterinary science is leading us and our pets down a path toward doggie cancer treatments and feline carpal tunnel surgeries. They're not human, so why use human medicine on them? Most animals are not anatomically complex. Did you know a cat has only four discrete parts? An alligator has sixteen parts! Learn the new science of animals! First course is $25. No commitment to remaining courses if not fully satisfied! National Dog and Cat School of New Medicine, ██████████, Hector, NV 89406.

UFO

CHINA HAS MADE CONTACT! They've had documented encounters for a thousand years longer than the U.S. has existed! China's own Babylon Working happened in the 8th century, and they've been trading with artificial life forms since the 15th century! What does the game of Go have to do with what these extraterrestrials want? Send $10 for the dossier with the frightening truth. Conspiracy Haus, ████████████████, New Sum, UT 84083.

Y2K-RAPTURE

STOCKING YOUR BUNKER with MREs? Meals Ready to Eat are last-generation time-wasters. The Pentagon has been hard at work on a brand new notion of battlefield chow. Fact: in a poisoned environment, whether it be radiation or poison gas released by the future robot overlords, opening the mouth for any reason is too risky. The mouth is an imperfect protector of your most vital areas. Introducing MIRs, Meals Introduced Rectally! Nutrition can be absorbed via the colon lining safely in a toxic environment. Let the most solid gasket on your body protect you while you eat! Studies have shown that combat effectiveness while eating improves 60% with MIRs! Only one flavor, because it doesn't matter! BIG SAVINGS RESULT! SILO SURVIVAL STORE, █████████, Hinckley, MT 59452.

LIFE IN A BUNKER can be hard. There's nobody you can really trust when the bombs fall and the pious vanish. Even a pet is just another mouth to feed in a world where the last can of pork and beans has already been made. You need human contact to maintain sanity and clarity, but what's a survivor to do? Imaginary Gary has a full line of imaginary friends you can get to know over a period of years! Each friend has a deep and complex biography that you can choose to reveal in any way you like, with our patented Getting To Know You Wheels! Line up the codes on the wheel and find out where your friend went to school, or the first time they had pizza! Spend the apocalypse working on your social skills and maintaining your cool. FREE catalog! IMAGINARY GARY, ████████, Shy Plains, IN 46952.

You will not . . . You must not . . .

TIRE

. . . or you'll miss these fascinating features!

You will not . . . you must not . . . TIRE*! The Seeker never tires of the truth, and Seekers read* TIRE*! We have articles and first-hand accounts of the strange and true in our world, presented every single month. Here's what you can expect to find in future issues of* TIRE:

∞ A dream is the mind's path out of the body. We always seem to know how to come back. But what happens when you dream too boldly, go too far, and can't find your way back? Allen Pfarning, D. D. S. examines Unconscious Wayfinding! *Nope, it'll be about tires.*

∞ From deep in the Amazon jungle come new snake venoms that pick the lock on the astral plane by paralyzing centers of the brain that lock in mortality and body supremacy! Dr. Wylene Gavel explores this new door to the Astral Plane! *Actually, it'll be about tires.*

∞ How did Shackleton keep every single man alive during his ill-fated Antarctic expedition from 1914-1917? He didn't! He was feeding on them! Tensor Fowley explains. *This part? It'll be about tires, too.*

∞ The race to build a perpetual motion machine is futile! We have to catch the one that's out there! Martine Gerelot reports. *You can read about some nice tires for it.*

THE JIT

Each month, we publish only the truth for Seekers. Don't delay, get your subscription to *TIRE* today!

128

NOTE ON THE 2016 PRINTING

In preparing this edition, I only added, never subtracting. I stripped in a tiny line at the bottom of the TOC, and added this section, as well as the now-standard "About Candle Light Press." The answer to the question "Why reprint a sixteen year old New Age magazine?" is, because Ruth said it was okay if I did. I'd put out an edition of *MEGACONTEMPLATIONS* in 2012, and *TIRE, June 2000* seemed like the next logical step. The *Fragmenta* series is all about reclaiming the past and providing context, as well as putting out every last thing I've ever done. One of these days, I'll start publishing Geometry homework.

These days I don't encounter many Jitters. In college, the joke around the Philosophy department was that if there wasn't some magic high-paying job waiting for us after graduation, we could at least throw on a sheet and start a cult. I think my cult moment has passed. Anymore, all the cults seem to be pseudo-Mormons and Quiverfull weirdos with loads of kids and wives. The fun cult moment, too, has passed. It's all about getting laid now. Jitters seem almost pleasant by comparison. They never really got enough divine information

from me to start wrecking other people's lives. They've spent most of their lives (and mine) waiting for more. There are still a couple websites trying to keep the flame alive. I'll let you find them.

There are so few Jitters left that I can't prank them anymore. It's like that cartoon aardvark dressing up as an ant. *What? I'm an ant!* The JIT moment is passing. I feel bad for anyone writing a straight JIT article now. Even I wouldn't believe I wasn't the author. There aren't many outlets to publish anything like that anymore. The magazines have all been reduced to Wicca or Astrology. And unless the article is all bullet points and starts with "You'll never guess . . . ," it doesn't have much of a shot on the Internet either. Magazines like *TIRE* were really prototypes for modern clickbait. They tried to put the whole spectrum of weirdness in every issue, often succeeding. Now you can buy them by the bag in antique stores.

If this book is to be dedicated to anyone, I think it has to be to the late Professor Jonathan A. Goldstein. When I was in grad school at the University of Iowa, I had the good fortune to know this amazing scholar. Fellow students in Classics were terrified to take a class from him, because his knowledge was so rich and deep. He would stop you on a dime if you were wrong.

He was a Biblical scholar of some renown. He wrote the Anchor Bible edition of the **Maccabees**. He was the kind of guy who said things about the Bible that everyone would nod along to. That's serious scholarship.

Once, he came into the TA office for a party and he sat at my desk. On the wall I had a page from the *Principia Discordia*, the one that says "Remember, King Kong died for your sins." Jonathan smiled and said to me, "King Kong didn't die for **my** sins." So this book is for Jonathan, who would have been appalled at it in the most informed and amusing way possible. I really should have shown him the original picture. I would have loved to hear what he had to say about the Baptists who felt my expulsion necessary.

Thanks should go out to Ruth Corley Watt for letting me retain the copyrights on this work. To her, the *TIRE* of her father isn't the *TIRE* of today, and I can see that. This work might even serve as the least annoying reminder of the man who raised her. She was a good sport to let me take over the freeway overpass that Jitters had been dropping bowling balls on me from for decades. She may have been born on third base, but that lady has plenty more turns at bat in her. — JIT

Fragmenta 8: TIRE, June 2000 was entirely written (yep, even the ads) and largely drawn by John Ira Thomas. Brian McNeil provided invaluable advice and helped pick nits in several drafts. Spot illos and modeling for ads and articles also done by Carter Allen, Kelli Grant, Will Grant, Austin Allen Hamblin, Thom Hotka, Jeremy Smith, Ulla the Dog, and Lonnie Vance. They did this because they are the BEST. Involuntary modeling for ads done by dead relatives, including my grandpa Buck Thomas and my great-grandpa Carl Seibel. All contents are copyright ©2016, John Ira Thomas and the artists. All rights are reserved. Country of 1st publication: The USA! No reproduction without permission. If you feed soda pop to rats, they will explode. Fnord.

About Candle Light Press

Candle Light Press exists to publish diverse and original works in both graphic and text formats. Our authors and artists all share a connection to the state of Iowa, where we first put our works into the world. From there, our books are available wherever books are sold. We are proud to re-present **TIRE, June 2000**, a document from an alternate timeline that's truer than you think.

www.candlelightpress.com

candle
light
press ™

1470 Walker Way, Coralville, IA 52241
ding@candlelightpress.com

www.ingramcontent.com/pod-product-compliance
Lightning Source LLC
Chambersburg PA
CBHW041606240626
47164CB00009B/199